MY MUM AND THE GRUESOME TWOSOME

Meg Harper

First published in Great Britain by
Lion Publishing plc 2001
This Large Print edition published by
BBC Audiobooks by arrangement with
Lion Publishing plc 2006

ISBN 10: 1 4056 6145 3
ISBN 13: 978 1 4056 6145 4

British Library Cataloguing in Publication **Data**

Harper, Meg, 19
My mum and the
gruesome
twosome / Meg
JLP

1711.723

Printed and bound in Great Britain by
Antony Rowe Ltd., Chippenham, Wiltshire

For my big sister, Janet,
with love

Contents

1

My Mum and Cute Carly

I can't believe it! I simply can't believe it! At her age! You'd think she'd know better. You'd really think she'd be more careful. After the way she goes on at us about being responsible and organized and making sensible choices. I mean, if you forget you've got PE and leave your kit at home, you get the third degree. And she's—I might as well put it bluntly—gone and GOT PREGNANT! There's nothing very organized and responsible about that, now, is there?

Ugh. It looks even worse written down, but I suppose I've got to get used to it. How could she? You'd think, seeing as Ben (my brother) is eleven and that I'm a teenager at long last, that she and Dad could get these things sorted. Apparently not. Mum had a bike accident before Christmas. That's her excuse.

'It seems to have messed up my fertility,' she said.

Huh! It seems to have messed up her brain! Well, I suppose that's possible; she did fracture her skull. Yikes, there's a thought. Perhaps she's losing it, like Gran. I can't cope. Pregnant and bonkers! Aargh!

Well, I let them know what I thought. That's why I'm stuck up here, typing away. Got sent to my room. I spent all last year, typing out my fury with my mum, my gran, my LIFE, and here I am again. I just can't believe it. I was getting on so well with Mum too. How could she do this to me? To all of us? We don't want a squalling brat of a baby, puking and pooing and chucking up all over the place. We want a life!

There's one thing for certain. Ben and I will have to change her nickname. She can't be Big Bum Mum (or BBM as we used to call her) any more. She'll have to be Big Tum Mum (BTM for short). She is going to be some shape. The mind boggles.

Tomorrow is Sunday. I wonder if they're going to tell Gran when she

2

comes for lunch. She'll probably have a heart attack. Maybe this is really a plot to get rid of her and, when she's gasped her last, they'll turn round and say it was a mistake. (It's a *big* mistake.) And I wonder if Mum's going to tell everyone at church? That's the trouble with being a part-time vicar. She does her whole life in public. Well, not quite all of it, but it's bad enough. It'll just confirm what they already think—that she's out of her tree. Good for the odd funeral or wedding but completely barking. Not only does she have multi-coloured hair and outrageous taste in clothes, but now she's been outed as a secret love-machine. Ouch!

Oh well, I suppose it can happen to anyone. Even famous people. Even prime ministers! *Very* ORGANIZED and RESPONSIBLE—*not!*

*   *   *

How wrong can you be? Gran is over the moon.

'Another baby! That's wonderful, dear. I always did think you should

3

have more.'

More? Am I surrounded by lunatics? Oh, all right, Gran hardly counts—she's been do-lally for years. But the people at church—you would have thought you could count on them for a bit of tight-lipped disapproval. No such luck. They're all delighted. They think it's so sweet. Suddenly, they've forgotten the spiky hair and the slogan-covered T-shirts. Mum's no longer that lunatic, lentil-eating lefty with 'views'. Suddenly, she's one of them—and all because she's having another baby. And you'd think they'd be a bit above all the nudging and winking and clapping Dad on the shoulder. But no. It's so embarrassing. Even the little old ladies are promising to knit matinee jackets. And this afternoon, a woman popped round with a pile of huge T-shirts for BTM. They say things like 'Room for Two' and 'It started with a kiss' and 'I'm not fat, I'm pregnant'. Huh! That last one's a joke. 'Cos she *is* fat. Well, her bum is.

I'm disappointed in Ben. He doesn't seem to care one way or the other.

He's never been one to get in a major flap about anything but I would have thought even he would get a bit worked up about this. I mean, what if the brat chews up his *Asterix* books? Or slobbers over his computer games? What then? He'd better not be turning into one of those awful teenage boys who do nothing but grunt. Maybe he's refusing to believe it'll really happen.

It'll happen all right. Now that she's told us, I'm remembering all the times in the last few weeks when Mum hasn't felt like breakfast. And she's developed a sudden passion for eating crisps. Very unlike her. Too full of additives. I should have realized. People have these mad cravings when they're pregnant. I read about it once in a magazine. Some women even eat coal! Ugh!

I haven't told anybody yet. It's too embarrassing. They'll find out at school before long anyway, because BTM keeps popping in to take assemblies and stuff. I shall die. I suppose I might tell Vicky tomorrow but I don't expect much sympathy from her. She likes babies. So my last hope is Chas—my best friend. He's away with his mum, so he missed the announcement at church. Surely, surely I can rely on him to understand? I wonder what his mum will think, the immaculate and oh-so-charming Mrs Peterson? I can't imagine this sort of thing ever happening to her. Now there's someone who is ORGANIZED and RESPONSIBLE. In fact, it makes you wonder how she had Chas. Maybe he was adopted.

*   *   *

Aargh! My life is falling apart. Chas rang this afternoon. His family had come home early and he wanted to bring this girl over to meet me. Bring THIS GIRL over to meet me? Chas is not a great socialite. He has two good friends—Ben and me—oh, and he gets on OK with Vicky too. So who on earth was this girl?

I soon found out. Carly. Her name's Carly. She's very small and delicate-looking with these huge brown eyes and lashes to die for. I hated her on sight. It's not that I'm jealous. Chas isn't into all that boyfriend/girlfriend stuff yet—well, I don't think he is. I just can't stand these really girlie girls who mince around, always pulling their skirts straight and taking care how they sit. To be fair, she was wearing jeans, but you know what I mean. She probably does ballet, for crying out loud.

Chas obviously couldn't see the problem.

'Hi Kate, Carly's moved into that barn conversion just down the road from us—remember I told you it had been sold at last?' (I didn't but never mind.) 'Well, Mum popped down there with a cake as soon as we got back . . .'

'She would,' I said rudely.

Chas looked puzzled but ploughed on. 'Anyway, she brought Carly back to meet me. Carly doesn't know anyone round here, of course, and I thought it'd be nice if she'd at least met one girl before she starts school tomorrow.'

Oh, fine, Chas Peterson, I thought. I see how it goes. You don't want to run around after her so you thought you'd dump on me. Fat chance, mate!

But Chas had that pleading look in his eyes, a look I can't resist.

'Well, take your coat off then,' I told the girl ungraciously. 'Come and meet my mum.'

That'd sort her out. Mum would have her life story out of her in five minutes and she'd feel all loved and wanted and stuffed with chocolate biscuits without me having to lift a finger. With a bit of luck, Mum would button-hole her for half-an-hour and Chas and I could sneak off to play darts with Ben.

In my dreams! It all started off all right. Mum was sprawled on the sofa recovering from a hectic afternoon playing rummy with Gran (who'd gone to sleep in the corner) but she perked up at the sight of someone fresh. Mum loves to get her teeth into a nice new member of the community. Before they know it, they're in the church choir or signed up to teach Sunday school.

She bustled off to put the kettle on while I asked all the usual boring questions. We had soon established that 'No, Carly hadn't wanted to move, yes, the house was all right, no, she didn't really like the countryside and the worst thing about being here was that she'd have to find a new dancing school.' What did I tell you? It's got to be ballet. It'd never be something decent like tap. (I rather fancy tap—all that stomping about.)

I'd just ground to a halt—Cute Carly didn't seem to want to know anything about me (she could probably tell my *pas de deux* wasn't up to much) when Mum returned with coffee and a plate of chocolate digestives. I sat back, relaxed and waited for her to take over. Suddenly . . .

'Oh, I'm sorry . . . I'll have to . . . it's the smell of the coffee . . .' she gasped and bolted out of the room.

'What's the matter with her?' said Ben, who had sneaked in with the chocolate biscuits—he can sniff out a packet at a hundred paces.

I shrugged and smiled sweetly at Carly. 'Who knows?' I said airily. 'Coffee?'

The sound of someone chucking-up violently in the downstairs loo drowned my words.

'Shut the door, will you?' I said to Chas casually.

'Hadn't you better go and see if she's all right?' he said, looking worried. 'She doesn't sound at all well.'

'Oh, she'll be fine,' I said, wanting to die. Cute Carly was looking appalled. She was frozen, biscuit halfway to her mouth. 'It's probably something she ate,' I added wickedly.

'It's not that, stupid,' said Ben. 'It's because she's pr . . .'

'Probably overtired,' I interrupted. 'It's hard work looking after Gran.'

'No, she's not. It's because she's going to . . .'

'To bed too late and getting up too early. She does tend to overdo things.'

I gave Ben one of my best 'shut-up-or-die' looks but he just stood there with his mouth hanging open, just like Gran, snoring away in the corner. Honestly, my family is a collection of freaks. They have no style. I couldn't bear the thought of Cute Carly being

10

one of the first to know what BTM had been up to.

At that moment, Mum returned. 'Sorry about that,' she said. 'You won't know, of course, but . . .'

'Hadn't you better go to bed, Mum?' I interrupted. 'You don't sound at all well.'

'No, I'm fine now. Really.'

At that moment, Gran woke with a terrific grunt which startled us all.

'Dear me, Jo,' she said. 'You look awful. Do sit down, dear. You can't be too careful, now you're . . .'

'Nearly forty?' I suggested desperately.

'Please don't interrupt, Kate,' said Gran haughtily. 'I wasn't going to say that at all. I was going to say that your mother really should be careful now that she's expecting another baby.'

Thank you, Gran. I love you too.

2

My Mum and the Belly-dancing

Someone up there is out to get me. I'm certain of it. Maybe this is all punishment for bad behaviour last year. I thought that was all forgiven and forgotten but now I'm not at all sure. When BTM *didn't* die in her bike accident (which was partly my fault), I was sure God had answered my prayers. But this! This is too much! Anyone who tries to tell me this is all for the good and that God really loves me can take a hike. This stinks!

Mum is sixteen weeks pregnant now. Somehow I've managed to get through the last eight weeks without slashing my wrists or being done for GBH. Mum has driven me round the bend. It was bad enough having a hyperactive mother, always getting us involved in some new project or other. It's even worse now that she's continually exhausted and bad-tempered. And sick! Yikes, she must have produced gallons of the stuff. How anyone who isn't eating anything except crisps and ginger tea can be quite so sick for quite so much of the time is beyond me. I thought it was supposed to be *morning* sickness. And that it stopped after twelve weeks. BTM has littered the house with books about pregnancy so I'm becoming an expert.

'Don't you know all this already?' I demanded, one day. 'It's eleven years since I did this,' she said. 'Things have changed.'

I snorted. 'Not that much. Babies still come out the same way, don't they?'

'That's not the point . . .' she began but I stalked off. I *do not* want to know the gory details. When it's my turn, kindly bang me on the head and wake me up when it's all over. When it's my turn . . . huh! What am I saying? If all this doesn't teach me not to bother having kids, then there's no hope for me. Becoming a nun would be more fun.

Ben, on the other hand (I am losing all sympathy for him), is intrigued. He's even been watching the videos BTM has brought home. There's one called 'Active Birth' which is beyond belief. I took one look and walked out. It's all writhing female bodies and sweat. It's no good—Chas really must be adopted. I just can't see Mrs Charming Peterson doing *anything* so undignified.

There's another one about breastfeeding which seems to consist entirely of close-ups of huge boobs. (Can't see the relevance to BTM—she isn't exactly well endowed in *that* department.) I'm amazed. Shouldn't these things be censored? Ben is probably watching them for all the wrong reasons. Even Chas has seen them. He did look a bit flushed and uncomfortable—though not half as much as when he burst in one evening to find BTM practising her belly-dancing. Belly-dancing! I ask you. At her age! Who does she think she is? A pop star? She'll have her belly-button pierced next. No! I didn't say it. Anything but that! She's got quite enough cheap tin tat hanging from her ears.

Of course, I can see what's happened. Being pregnant is the new project—when she's got the energy that is. In between her times with her head down the loo she's into all this with a vengeance. I suppose it's mildly more normal than usual. Keeping a pig was her last craze. And before that it was abseiling.

I worried about it for days. Should I say nothing and let her belly-dance the baby to death? I was tempted, I admit it, I *was* tempted. I scoured the pregnancy books but the best I could come up with was that high-impact sport should be avoided. Well, it would be high-impact if she fell over—I'd fear for the floorboards—so in the end I tackled Dad. I didn't fancy getting my head snapped off, which is all too likely with BTM at the moment.

Dad has been suspiciously quiet about all this and so he should be. After all, he *is* the guilty party. 'Course I can understand the temptation for BTM—he's still very presentable at

15

forty-two, even though his ponytail is beginning to go grey. He's not like her at all. She's short and pear-shaped. He's tall and slim and agile-looking. Quite like me, in fact. Just a pity he's a hairdresser. I do get fed up with all the jokes.

Anyway, I waited till he was drying his hair and then attacked while he couldn't escape.

'Kate, don't you think you ought to knock before you come marching into our bedroom?' he protested.

This was so unlike him that for a moment I was thrown. Soon recovered though.

'Oo-oh!' I quipped. 'Getting modest, are we? It's a bit late for that. We all know what you and Mum have been up to!'

'Kate . . .' he said warningly. Huh! If he doesn't like me talking about it, he should be more careful. I sat down on the bed. He picked up the hairdryer as if it was a weapon.

'Dad, about this belly-dancing . . .' I began.

'What . . . ? I can't hear you!'

'The belly-dancing,' I shouted. He wasn't going to escape that easily. 'Isn't it a bit dangerous?'

'What? For your mum?'

'No, for the baby.'

Resignedly, he flicked the off-switch. 'Apparently not. It's been done for centuries. Helps prepare all the right bits for the birth. And your mum is having lessons with someone who knows what they're doing.'

'Oh. So there's no chance of her stopping?'

' 'Fraid not. OK?'

No, it was not OK. The thought of my mother gyrating round the lounge for another five months or so, all the time getting bigger and bigger, was too much. Someone was bound to find out.

And they did, of course. And it wasn't just Chas either. I could have coped with him—I think.

It was the end of the Easter holidays. I was slobbing around in my bathrobe, eating a huge pile of toast and listening to Radio 1. I don't know where Ben was. Probably plugged into his computer. He has to be surgically

17

removed these days unless he's hungry. Anyway, nobody rushed to the door when the bell rang, so the second time I groaned and went myself.

On the doorstep stood Chas (scruffy sweatshirt and jeans) and Cute Carly (immaculate designer tracksuit). I was suddenly very aware of a) the hot chocolate stains on my bathrobe and b) the toast crumbs stuck all round my mouth. I scrubbed at them with my sleeve. Mistake.

'Oh,' said Chas, taking in my appearance. 'We were going to ask if you wanted to come on a bike ride.'

Oh we were, were we? And since when had Cute Carly been one of us?

'Come in,' I said woodenly. 'I'll be ready in a minute.'

Chas was just about to take Carly into the kitchen when I remembered the mess I'd left it in—all last night's washing up was still spread everywhere because I'd kindly offered to load the dishwasher (I do have my forgiving moments) and then forgot.

'In here,' I said hastily and flung open the door of the lounge. Second mistake. Even Chas, who now knows to expect absolutely anything from my mum, looked startled and Carly's eyes were on stalks.

BTM has got herself one of those crop tops people wear for aerobics—a natty little number in black. She was wearing that and a flowing Indian cotton skirt hitched over her bump (which now that I come to think of it was looking very large) and was writhing away to some tuneless music. Serves me right for having the radio on so loud that I couldn't hear it.

Chas was the first to recover. 'Hello Jo,' he said and blushed. 'Sorry to interrupt your . . . ?'

'Belly-dancing,' said BTM cheerily. 'You're into dancing, aren't you Carly? Is this your sort of thing?'

Carly appeared to have been struck dumb. She seemed to be fixated on my mother's armpits. I felt myself going hot and cold all over. I'm used to BTM and the way she won't shave anything, least of all her armpits. She likes to 'celebrate the fully feminine figure' as she puts it. I swear she actually enjoys having rolls of flesh round her bum.

'Mum, is it OK if I go on a bike ride with Chas and Carly?' I said quickly. (I didn't like the way those names seemed to fit together.) 'I forgot about the dishwasher but I could do it later.'

Mum fixed me with a steely eye. 'Do it now,' she said. 'If I have to face all that congealed chicken curry, I shall throw up.'

It's unbelievable, isn't it? How can she say these things in front of someone like Carly?

'Oh Mum . . .' I groaned.

'It's all right, Kate,' said Chas. 'I'll do it. You get ready.'

I looked at him as if he'd suddenly sprouted two heads. Chas is a nice lad—let's face it, he's my best friend—but domesticated? No. I had a sudden unpleasant suspicion that there was someone in the room that he was trying to impress—and it wasn't Mum or me.

'Sure you know how?' I snorted and left him to it. I was pretty certain Cute Carly wouldn't offer to give him a hand.

Ben was in the bathroom, staring at

20

himself in the mirror like a mouldering zombie.

'Do you ever brush your hair?' I said, pushing past him.

'Kate, I'm getting spots,' he said. 'It's not fair. I'm only eleven.'

'Too many chocolate biscuits,' I retorted unsympathetically. I looked in the mirror at his pasty face. 'Ugh! Be careful or you'll turn out like BTM. Fancy a bike ride? Fresh air is good for spots.'

'With Chas?'

'Yes . . . and . . .'

'Not Carly?'

' 'Fraid so.'

Ben looked at me sideways. 'You don't think he fancies her, do you?'

'Who? Chas?' I said with an attempt at a laugh. 'No—he's not interested in girlfriends. Not yet.'

Ben frowned. 'It's got to happen sometime, you know, Kate.'

'Ben, you sound about ninety. Shut up!'

'It's happened to me already.'

'What? What are you talking about?'

'I've started fancying girls. That's

why I don't want spots.'

My jaw hit the floor. 'Are you serious?'

' 'Course I am. I fancy Nicky Stevens, Zoe Cuthbert and Danielle Aston. But Suzie Ellis is the best. Phwoar!'

'Ben!' I was speechless.

He grinned sheepishly and shrugged. 'So don't be too sure about Chas, that's all,' he said.

I wasn't. That was the trouble. I wasn't—and I didn't like it.

*   *   *

I didn't enjoy the ride. I spent the whole time on the look-out for signs but Chas seemed happy to divide his time equally between the three of us. He larked around with Ben, was his usual self with me, and with Carly . . . ? Well, he did seem very careful to say the right thing—but he's shy and quiet until he gets to know *anyone* properly. Anyway, it made me cross. We couldn't have our usual relaxed time. I kept hoping Carly would get tired and want to go home but she kept up with us easily. Must be all that dancing. She *does* do ballet—and jazz. When we stopped for a snack, she droned on for ages about how all the dancing schools round here are rubbish. And then she said something which really made my blood boil.

'Does your mum fancy herself as a dancer then? I couldn't believe it. Belly-dancing! What does she think she looks like?'

I could feel my face going almost purple with rage. Let's get this straight. Only Ben and I are allowed to be rude about BTM. Anyone else—instant death. OK, so she really gets up my nose sometimes with her wacky ideas and, boy, can she be embarrassing, but basically she's the best mum in the world and I wouldn't want her any other way.

I caught Ben's eye. I could see he was furious too. All his freckles were standing out because his face goes white when he's angry.

'Actually,' I said tightly, 'she's only dancing because it's good for you when you're pregnant. Normally she's into far more exciting things like abseiling.'

'And scuba-diving,' said Ben.

'And kick-boxing,' added Chas.

I flashed Chas my best smile. So he *was* still on our side. BTM has never done kick-boxing in her life, as far as I know!

'Yes,' I said nonchalantly. 'She's usually far too busy enjoying life to put too much time into just one thing.'

'Well, that was obvious,' snapped Carly. 'You could see she didn't really know what she was doing.'

That was it. This meant WAR. I'm as happy to love my neighbour as the next person (Mum's forever quoting that bit of the Bible at us) but there are limits! Unfortunately, I was so outraged that my mind went completely blank. Not so Ben.

'Come on,' he said. 'I'm still hungry. Let's go home. I'm sure you're right about Mum, Carly. Of course, she hasn't had as much practice as you.'

Ben held out his hand politely to help Carly up. Not suspecting anything, she grasped it. One deft twist of the wrist and she went sprawling—

headlong into a neat row of cowpats.

'Oh dear, Carly,' said Ben, as Chas rushed to the rescue. 'What *do* you think you look like?'

'Don't pretend that was an accident, Ben Lofthouse!' Carly spat, struggling to her feet.

Ben shrugged but couldn't help blushing.

'I think I'd better take Carly home,' said Chas quietly. 'That was pretty mean.'

I was speechless. The traitor! So la-di-da little Carly had to be escorted home, did she, just because nasty old Ben pushed her in the cow-poo? What about her being so rude about BTM? What about *that*?

'But Chas . . .' I started.

Chas just looked at me. I could see there was no point in arguing.

*   *   *

Ben and I cycled home in silence.

'Sorry, Kate,' he said, as we put our bikes away. 'I didn't think Chas'd do that.'

25

'It's OK. I'd have done the same as you did if I could've got my brain together. It doesn't matter about Chas.'

But it did matter. I couldn't believe he'd suddenly changed sides like that. I was gutted. Totally and utterly gutted. And worse was to come.

Mum was sitting on a stool in the kitchen staring into space. She looked very odd—sort of pale and distant.

'Are you all right?' I asked hesitantly. It was then that I remembered. She'd been going that morning for a scan, to check that the baby was growing all right and everything. 'Shall I make you a cup of tea? Is the baby . . . is the baby all right?' I suddenly knew that however much I resented this baby, I would feel terrible if something had happened to it.

Ben was right beside me. 'Mum,' he said and pawed at her shoulder. 'Mum, tell us. Is there anything wrong with the baby?'

'Oh, everything's all right,' she said briskly, pulling herself together. 'Everything's fine. It's just that it isn't one baby . . .'

We must have looked absolutely appalled.

She laughed weakly. 'That's right. You've guessed it. It's not one baby. It's two!'

3

My Mum has a Crisis

Twins! Yikes, weren't things bad enough? Even Ben's looking worried now and I'm convinced Dad's hair has gone greyer overnight. Only Mum, after the initial shock, seems remotely keen on the idea.

'But it's really exciting,' she keeps saying. 'I feel really special.'

Is she real? She's already bought yet another book. *Twins or More* it's called. Apparently we've had a lucky escape. It could have been triplets or even quads. The older you get, the more likely it is.

Dad's not impressed at all. Last night he and Mum had a row, so things must be bad. They virtually never argue. It was terrible. Ben actually unplugged himself from his PC to listen. It was all about whether they should have tests to see if the babies might be handicapped. Apparently, there's more chance with twins. Yikes—as if there wasn't enough to worry about.

'I don't like this, Kate,' said Ben. He looked very forlorn. I suddenly felt very sorry for him. Raging hormones and raging parents too! I put my arm round him.

'Don't worry. They'll be OK in the morning. You know what they always say to us—"Don't let the sun go down on your anger." Come on. Let's go and raid the biscuit tin.'

Ben shook his head. 'You've forgotten my spots, Kate,' he said.

Well, that's it, I thought. If Ben's given up biscuits then this really is the end of the world.

*　　　*　　　*

I lay awake half the night agonizing. Knowing Mum she'll probably pray

28

about it and 'leave it in the hands of God'. It's OK for some! It was quite a relief to go to school, despite the fact that my eyes felt like I'd been swimming in bleach. The chances are the babies will be absolutely fine—but even so, the thought of *two* of them! Nothing is ever going to be the same again. And I liked my life as it was. I've always adored Dad, Ben is great as little brothers go, I've got two fantastic friends (most of the time anyway!) and I've been getting on really well with Mum recently. And since Mum's accident I've felt differently about God—as if he might actually be listening to my prayers. Until now.

And of course, in the back of my mind, there's always the problem with Chas. I feel guilty even thinking about it but it kept me awake too. It ought to be unimportant compared with what's happening to our family. But I can't help it. Does he fancy Carly? Does he?

I was looking forward to seeing him. It was three days since that awful bike ride and I'd only seen him briefly at church. He heard about the twins there, of course, and made all the right, sympathetic noises, but I hadn't had a chance to talk to him properly. We're in the same tutor group so usually manage a quick chat first thing. We catch up with each other at lunch time and he often comes home with me after school. Not just because of me, of course—he's Ben's friend too. That's really how I got to know him.

Anyway, for the first time since he had chicken pox, Chas wasn't in our tutor room waiting for me. Could he be ill? I hung around, biting my nails and pretending I was interested in all the work stuck on the notice-boards. I get on OK with the others in my group, but no one's a real buddy. I was just imagining Chas lying squashed in a ditch when the door flew open.

'Kate!' It was Vicky. She's in a different tutor group from me. 'Kate, I've just seen Chas and he's . . .'

At that moment, Chas himself appeared in the doorway, just ahead of our tutor.

'Hi Kate,' he said breathlessly, gave

me a quick grin and then, for some unknown reason, blushed.

Vicky looked at him oddly. 'I'll tell you later, Kate,' she said. 'Gotta go.' And she was off.

'You OK?' I asked, as Chas squeezed by to get to his desk.

'Fine,' he said quickly and then it was time for registration. What had Vicky been going to say? And why was Chas so late? I could hardly wait to see Vicky later.

My first lesson dragged horribly. As soon as it was over, I flew down the corridor to grab Vicky before Maths.

'Well?' I demanded. 'What was all that about earlier?'

Vicky looked around quickly and lowered her voice. 'Chas . . . he cycled into school with Carly. They were hanging round the bike racks chatting when I came in. Is he going out with her or something?'

I suddenly felt very cold. 'Of course not . . . well, I don't think so, anyway. He hasn't said anything. I was going to tell you though. On Friday, he turned up with her and wanted to go on a bike ride with us.'

'Did you go?'

'Of course.'

'Was it awful?'

'What d'*you* think? We ended up having this sort of row.'

'What about?'

'Oh, she had a go at Mum, so Ben kind of pushed her in some cow-pats— and Chas took her side. I couldn't believe it!'

'Hmm, he's been a bit odd all holidays.'

'No, he hasn't! He's been fine.'

'You just haven't noticed, Kate. You've been too busy worrying about this baby.'

Baby! Yikes, I hadn't told Vicky.

'Vicky, wait a minute! Never mind all that. I haven't told you. You're never going to believe this. It's not just one baby any more. It's twins!'

Vicky sat down hard on her chair. 'Twins! Kate, that's awful. First Chas and Carly and now twins! Poor you.'

Suddenly, I didn't want her sympathy. I was angry. 'What d'you mean—poor me? What d'you mean—

Chas and Carly? Don't tell me you think he fancies her too! I've had enough of that from Ben!'

'Oh Kate. Of course he does.' Vicky rolled her eyes. 'And you think I'm jealous?'

'Well, aren't you?'

'No. We're just good friends. Always have been.'

Vicky raised her eyebrows. I buried my head in my bag. Jealous? Me? Are you kidding? Of course I was. I was as green as a little man from Mars.

*   *   *

Chas was waiting for me at break time.

'Kate,' he said, 'I need to talk to you.'

'Don't force yourself,' I snapped, preparing to march off with Vicky. But Vicky had mysteriously disappeared.

Chas flushed. 'Kate, don't be like that. Is this just because I cycled in with Carly? I don't get it. Why can't I be friends with Carly *and* you? Can't we just be one big gang?'

'Are you serious? Couldn't you tell from that bike ride? She doesn't like me.' To my horror, I could feel tears pricking at my eyes which were still sore from lack of sleep. 'Look, Chas, I don't want to talk about it right now. I'm tired and I'm fed up.'

'I know, Kate—I know how you feel about the babies,' he said,

'No, you don't. You've always wanted a brother or a sister.'

'But Kate . . .' I could hear him, calling after me, as I stomped away. 'Kate, wait! I need to talk to you.'

*   *   *

I was sorry by lunch time, of course. I found him where I knew he'd be, in the library. He was nose-down in a *Far Side* collection.

'Chas, do you ever do any proper reading?' I groaned.

'What, you mean *Goosebumps?*' He grinned.

I biffed him. It was impossible to be cross with him for long. 'You know I don't read all that . . .'

'Don't say it,' he warned. 'The librarian's watching. Come on, let's get out of here.'

But when we were out in the corridor things got awkward again.

'No Carly?' I enquired lightly.

'Gym club.'

'Of course.'

'Look . . .' We both spoke together.

'After you,' said Chas.

'No, after you.'

He waited.

I sighed. 'Oh, all right then. I'm sorry I was so grumpy at break time. What was it you wanted to say to me?'

Chas blushed. He was making a habit of it. 'It's about Carly actually.' He hesitated then went for the jugular. 'D'you think I should ask her out?'

I am going to die, I thought. I suddenly felt as if my insides were bungee jumping. I couldn't move.

'Well,' I said, and I was amazed to hear my voice coming out perfectly normally. 'Doesn't that depend on how you feel about her?' (Impressive, hey? Think I'd make a good shrink?)

'But I don't *know* how I feel about her.'

'Well, I shouldn't bother then.

35

Anyway, I thought you weren't into all that sort of stuff yet.'

'I wasn't but . . .' His cheeks were flaming *again*!

'But now you think you are?' First Ben studying his spots in the mirror and now this! 'Tell you what,' I said. 'Why don't you ask Ben what he thinks? He fancies half the girls in his class.'

'You're joking?'

'I am not. Try him. Seriously.'

Chas suddenly looked very relieved. 'That's a brilliant idea, Kate. Thanks. That's a real help. I hadn't thought of asking him.'

I shook my head in bewilderment. Had the world gone mad? My spotty little brother as agony aunt?

'Anyway,' said Chas, 'what's wrong with your eyes? You haven't been crying, have you?'

I shook my head and explained why I'd hardly had any sleep. Not that I mentioned Cute Carly, of course.

'Your mum and dad were having a row?' Chas was amazed.

'I know, I know, it's unheard of—

36

well, almost. It was about whether they should have tests done on the babies.'

'They aren't going to, are they?'

He sounded so appalled that my temper snapped again. I let rip. He deserved it. Ask Cute Carly out? How dare he even think of going out with a prissy little thing like that?

'Well, why on earth shouldn't they? It's all very well for you,' I stormed. 'It's all so easy from the outside, isn't it? But this is our whole family that's being messed up. And you think it's so simple!'

'But I thought they didn't believe in abortion—so what's the point of having any tests?'

'I don't care what they believe, I don't care what you believe, I'm just fed up with the whole business and I can't stand people who think they know what's best for everyone else!'

Chas was getting angry too. 'Look, I hardly said a word. I never said I knew best. I just don't think you should keep on and on about *your* life being messed up. It's always you, you, you, isn't it? What about the poor babies? When do

37

they get a look-in?'

'That's not fair, Chas Peterson! How would you like it if . . .' I was beginning to cry and I hadn't got a tissue. I must have looked dreadful, pasty-white, red-eyed with tiredness and streaming with tears. I saw a small, dainty figure hurrying towards us. It was Cute Carly, of course.

'Oh just shut up!' I snapped. 'And don't bother to wait for me after school.' Then I turned and ran.

*   *   *

Vicky did a good mopping up job. She even coaxed me into wearing some of the make-up she'd got in her bag.

'If you want him back, you'd better start making a bit of an effort,' she said.

She didn't understand. 'It's not like that,' I said. It's never been like that. Not with me and Chas. You know that.'

'Then why are you so upset?'

'I don't know. I'm probably just tired.'

'Well, you look like something the

cat's dragged in, so you'd better bung some of this on.'

I felt better by the end of school. We had games last period, which I'm good at, especially hockey. Cute Carly, I was pleased to see, was fast but nervous. You have to be a bit of an animal for hockey.

I tried not to look as Chas chatted with Carly by the bike racks. Any moment now they'd cycle off together. Imagine my surprise when Chas waved her off and ran to intercept me.

'I thought I told you . . .' I began.

'Don't start, Kate,' he begged. 'Just stay cool, all right?'

'OK,' I said testily. 'So what d'you want?'

He snorted. 'I *want* to cycle home with Carly if you must know. But my mum rang school and says I've got to go to your house. She's there and she's making tea for all of you.'

'What? What on earth for?' The idea of Mrs Charming Peterson, always so immaculate in her navy blue and her hairband, finding her way round our chaotic kitchen, was beyond belief.

And then the penny dropped.

'Mum!' I gasped. 'There's something wrong with Mum!' The last time Mrs Peterson had organized our lives Mum had been dicing with death on her bike—this time I was sure it was to do with the babies.

Chas grabbed my arm. I think he thought I was going to faint. I must say I did feel very odd. My insides were bungee jumping again.

'Don't panic,' he said. 'Mum just said that the doctor's been and that he's sent your mum to bed. My mum called by when he was there, so the easiest thing to do was to stay and sort everything out.'

'Yes,' I said. 'It's Monday. Dad's got a students' night at the salon, so he'll be late.'

'Anyway, you're stuck with me, I'm afraid. Sorry.'

How could he be so stupid? At a time like this, he was the one person in the world I wanted!

'That's OK,' I said sheepishly. 'I think I can put up with you.'

We walked home, Chas pushing his

bike, talking about what might be wrong. I'd done enough reading to have a pretty good idea.

'She's probably threatening to miscarry,' I said.

'Oh. Does that mean she might lose the babies?'

I nodded.

'Well . . .' Chas looked sideways at me.

'Don't say it. Don't say anything about that being a good thing.'

'I wasn't going to.'

'Or about that suiting me perfectly.'

'Well, you did say . . .'

'I don't care what I said. Just imagine how I'm going to feel if she loses them. I'll feel like a murderer.'

'But it isn't your fault . . .'

'No, but I haven't exactly helped. I haven't exactly made Mum feel good about it . . .' I was beginning to cry again. This had been one of the most horrible days of my life. I blew my nose.

'You were right, Chas. All I've thought about is myself.'

Mrs Peterson is not my favourite person. In fact, I'd go so far as to say that if she weren't Chas's mum, I'd be happy if she suffocated in her own face-powder. She fusses and she gushes. Mrs Charming Peterson. That's what Ben and I have always called her. What BTM sees in her is beyond me. It's probably what comes of being a part-time vicar. She has to see the good in everyone.

Anyway, when we burst through the back door into the kitchen, I couldn't believe my eyes. The place was gleaming—and there in the middle of it, suitably togged up in a navy and white butcher's apron, was Mrs Peterson, *scrubbing out our waste bin*! I don't think anyone has thought of doing that since it was bought—and we haven't all died of food poisoning.

'There!' she said. 'That's that little job done.' She looked flushed but pleased. She tucked a stray hair into her hair-band and adjusted her pearls. 'A drink, children?' she asked, as if she was offering us sherry. 'And some shortbread?'

I noticed the home-made shortbread, cooling on a rack. Had she been here for a week? The whole room was full of the most delicious smell of something simmering in the oven. You had to hand it to her—she was a worker. I could never quite get my head round the fact that she was a farm-manager's wife and had a husband who spent half his life covered in pig-poo.

I tried to be polite. 'That'd be lovely, Mrs Peterson,' I said. 'But how's Mum?'

'In bed. You can go up and see her as long as you're very quiet. The doctor says it may be nothing to worry about—this sort of thing doesn't always mean there's something wrong . . .'

'What sort of thing?'

Mrs Peterson looked flustered. 'Kate, I don't think we should . . . not with Charles here. Girls' talk, you know.' She gave a high little laugh. 'Better ask your mother.'

I caught Chas's eye. He was

desperately trying not to smirk. I'd told him as much as I knew about miscarriages on the way home. But it wasn't really funny. I mean, poor boy! Was it surprising he didn't know whether to ask a girl out? He hadn't even known the facts of life until I'd told him. And he lives on a farm! He'd just kind of assumed it was different for humans. Obviously couldn't imagine his mum . . . Maybe he thinks he's adopted too.

'Where's Ben?' I asked, to spare Mrs Charming's blushes.

Immediately, she was all fussy concern. 'Poor Ben! He's in his room. Very grumpy. He must be sickening for something—he won't eat any of my shortbread.'

'Oh, he's just lovesick,' I said and enjoyed Mrs Peterson's puzzled frown. 'I'll pop up and see Mum, if that's all right.'

On the way, I went to the loo. Or I tried to anyway. Ben was gazing into the mirror again. This time he was armed with a comb and a can of hair mousse.

44

'I don't believe it,' I said. 'Are you auditioning for a boy band?'

Ben glowered at me in the mirror.

'Oh, good expression,' I said. 'Nice pout. Very cool.'

'D'you think I should ask Dad to do something different with my hair?' he demanded.

I nearly fell over backwards into the bath.

'Mrs Peterson's right,' I said. 'No appetite. Complete personality change. Call an ambulance. This condition is serious.'

'Oh shut up,' Ben growled. 'I mean it. What d'you think?'

'I think . . .' I chewed the end of my finger thoughtfully. 'I think . . . yes—shave the lot off. Can't think why you didn't do it years ago.'

He squirted me with the mousse.

'Go and talk to Chas,' I said, flicking it back in his face. 'You were quite right. His hormones have gone bonkers too.'

*   *   *

BTM was lying in bed, reading. She looked glum. Even her spiky hair had drooped.

'Well?' I whispered.

She patted the bed and I sat down close to her. 'Sorry you've got lumbered with Mrs Charming,' she said. 'She was just passing.'

I shrugged. 'Doesn't matter. What about the babies?'

She smiled wanly. 'It may be nothing. Just a few twinges and a drop or two of blood. If anything else is going to happen, we'll soon know.'

'Shouldn't you be in hospital?'

She shook her head. 'It's very common to miscarry, even at this stage. There's nothing they can do. I may lose one baby, I may lose both.'

I didn't ask her how she felt about that. How would anyone feel? However difficult it was going to be, she wanted those babies.

'Kate,' she said and reached out for my hand. 'I know you're not happy about all this . . .'

'I'm sorry,' I said. 'I . . .'

'Shh. It's OK. You don't have to say

anything. But I just wondered . . . I know you'd find it difficult . . .' She paused.

What on earth was she going to say? My imagination went wild. Was she going to ask me to be present at the birth? Or maybe give up my room and share with Ben? (We hadn't quite sussed where the babies were going to sleep yet.)

I said. 'Go on . . .'

'I just wondered if you'd mind praying for the babies? Now, I mean. With me. Because your dad isn't here and I'd like . . .' She stopped. She sounded very choked. 'Even part-time vicars need a bit of help with their prayers sometimes.'

I nearly cried. Awkwardly, I kissed her on the cheek.

'Of course,' I said, pulling myself together and feeling horribly responsible. And horribly mixed-up. I wasn't too happy with God at the moment. Could I really pray for the babies to be OK? In all honesty? Would it work? I looked at Mum's face. It was tight and anxious. Chas's words came back to me. I just don't think you should keep on and on about your life being messed up. It's always you, you, you, isn't it?

I sighed. I didn't really have a choice, did I? So I held Mum's hand and prayed.

4

My Mum and the Girlfriend

Mum and the babies were all right after all. Somehow I never got round to writing that down. In fact, it's been weeks since I've needed to pour out my heart on this machine. It was strange about that false alarm. At the time it was awful but once BTM was better again, I felt much happier about everything. Thinking that she might be going to lose the babies suddenly made me realize I was quite excited about them after all. I mean, twins! It doesn't happen to everyone, does it? And I suppose it made me feel better about

Chas and Carly too—for a while, anyway. I mean, I was so relieved that BTM was OK that nothing else seemed so important. BTM was remarkably smug about it all, though she did have the decency to thank me for praying with her. 'All things work together for the good of those who love him,' she said. By 'him', she means God. I wish she'd get out of this tendency to quote the Bible at me. I'll never get used to it. Anyway, I'm not so sure about that bit. I'll wait to be convinced.

At least Chas hasn't asked Carly out *yet*—and it's been weeks since he wanted my advice. Maybe Ben told him not to. Or maybe he's a complete wimp. They still hang around a lot together and she still gazes up at him with her big gooey eyes and there're still heaps of rumours flying round about them, but apart from that— nothing. It's everyone else who's driven me back to the keyboard. BTM. Dad. Ben. Good old, predictable little brother Ben. Who would believe he could change so much? And with no warning! His voice hasn't even broken yet!

He did have his hair cut and I must say, it does look good. But the time he takes over styling it! It's incredible. He's gone from being Headlice Hotel to Mousse Maniac almost overnight. Maybe Dad was like that as a boy. Maybe Ben's going to be a hairdresser too? Huh! Fat chance of that, surely? Yikes, I just don't know any more. Anything could happen.

The other evening, I wanted a bath. The light was on in the bathroom and I could hear giggling. The door wasn't locked so I went in. Ben and Chas were standing in front of the mirror, shirts open to the waist, posing. Quick as a flash, they covered themselves up. Chas even turned his back.

'Oh, really,' I groaned. 'What is the matter with you two? I've seen it all before, you know. We only went swimming on Saturday, remember? What were you doing? Inspecting your six-packs or looking for hairs on your chests?'

There was a horrible silence. Chas didn't turn round. Ben went an

50

interesting beetroot colour. I'd obviously hit the nail on the head.

I burst out laughing. 'Go on then,' I said. 'Which was it? Or was it both?'

Ben lost his temper. 'Go away, Kate. I'm fed up with you always laughing at me. And knock before you come in, in future. You're just jealous 'cos no one fancies you.'

I laughed myself silly. 'Oh, come on, Ben. Lighten up. What are you on about? I suppose you're the super-stud of Year 6? In your dreams!'

'Well, that's where you're wrong, Miss Clever Clogs,' snarled Ben. 'And if you don't believe me, ask BTM. Suzie Ellis is coming to lunch on Sunday. So there!'

Now it was my turn to look uncomfortable. I stood there, absolutely speechless, feeling ridiculous. Everyone was moving on, except me. The boys nearly fell over themselves laughing. In the end, Chas took pity on me. 'Oh, come on, Kate,' he said. 'Don't look like that. It's not the end of the world. And she's a really nice girl.'

'Have you met her?'

'Yes.'

'Where?'

'Oh, you know . . . around.'

'Around where?'

'Oh, the park, the shops . . . why? What's it to you?'

I was suddenly feeling incredibly left out. My eyes were smarting. I sniffed angrily.

'Oh, it doesn't matter,' I snapped. 'But I can tell you one thing, Ben. There's no way BTM'll let you go out with her. Not when you're only eleven!'

Ben shrugged. 'So? We see each other at school, don't we? And you're always hanging around with Chas. Why can't I do that with Suzie?'

'That's different. It's not like Chas and I . . .' I stopped. I wasn't at all sure *what* the score was with Chas any more. I'm still not. Ever since Carly appeared on the scene, nothing has been quite the same between us. For months he's been my best friend—but I don't know if he is any longer.

'Oh, get back to counting your hairs,' I said scornfully, and slammed out of the bathroom. Then I went to my room and sulked.

*　　　*　　　*

Sunday came and so did Suzie—and Gran, of course, much to my secret delight. She always comes to Sunday lunch. I think BTM arranges these things deliberately. The first time we had lunch with the Petersons we had to take Gran. I reckon she thinks that anyone who can cope with Gran can't be too bad. I wondered if Suzie would pass the test.

She didn't come to church with us which I thought was a bad sign. Ben and I aren't totally signed-up members of the God squad but we both still trot obediently along to church. Apart from anything else, it's quite good fun.

'Your Suzie's not coming to church then?' I asked.

'No,' said Ben. 'She doesn't go to church, as such.'

I smirked. BTM wouldn't be too impressed with that.

'She goes to the Salvation Army.'

I did a quick double take. Did that

53

mean she would turn up in a bonnet playing a tambourine? I'd been imagining one of these wannabe pop-stars—all fashion and pose; I'd been too sulky to ask for any details.

'It's OK, Kate,' said Ben, suddenly sounding very grown-up. 'You'll like her—honest. She isn't like Carly.'

Huh! I thought. I shall definitely hate her. I'll force myself.

But the awful truth is that Suzie is nice. Ben clearly has far better taste than Chas. I could see the attraction immediately. She's on the cuddly side (so is Ben—he takes after BTM) and has far too good a figure for an eleven year old. She has curly red hair and one of those pink and white faces that blushes ever so easily. Very pretty in an old-fashioned sort of way. She was wearing clean jeans and a smart fleece and looked . . . well . . . normal.

I am not a miserable old so-and-so really, and was quite prepared to be forgiving. I mean, is it her fault my little brother has turned into Casanova overnight? She didn't show any signs of wanting to whisk him off for a quick snog; in fact, she behaved just as Vicky does when invited to lunch. Friendly, polite and talkative. Very.

That was the one problem. Boy, did she talk. I thought my mum was chatty but really—Suzie could chat for England! BTM says she probably can't get a word in edgeways at home. I think she's only interested in Ben because he's someone she can sound off at. We soon knew all about her mum (who's too busy to go out to work) and her dad (who's a vet) and her six younger brothers and sisters. Six! I ask you! Then there were her pets and her aunts and uncles (who are always having tiffs with her mum), not to mention her grandparents who are all still alive and definitely kicking. It must be a real challenge to fit Ben in.

Mum and Dad and Gran and Ben hung on her every word. It was as if she was holding court. All my bad feelings began to come back. Dad looked positively entranced by the lively little lady.

It was when we got on to babies the trouble began.

'Seven children—and you're the oldest!' said BTM, exploiting one of Suzie's rare pauses. 'How does your mum cope?'

'Well, I help a lot,' said Suzie. 'I often give Freddie—he's the baby—his bottle, and bath the little ones and stuff.'

'Oh,' said BTM. I saw her stiffen a little. 'Your mum doesn't breastfeed then?'

I was instantly on Suzie's side. BTM has a thing about breastfeeding; she thinks the whole world should do it, preferably until the baby is five years old.

'No,' said Suzie. 'She couldn't do it with me and never bothered to try again.'

'Oh,' said BTM and the room seemed to chill by several degrees. 'I wonder why she thought she couldn't do it?'

I could see Dad trying to catch Mum's eye and Ben was beginning to twitch. But Suzie carried on blithely.

'Oh, not enough milk or something,' she said.

56

Now, I've already had several arguments about this with Mum. I mean, I know breastfeeding is wonderful and it fills the baby full of antibodies against everything from the common cold to the bubonic plague, but there are times when it's just not going to be possible. And I think having twins is one of them. I mean, apart from anything else, you're bound to have to feed them both at the same time—and how do you do that without revealing all you've got to the world in general? (Not that BTM's got very much of course—or she didn't have until she got pregnant.) It just isn't *decent*. How am I going to feel if I come in from school with Chas and she's sitting there baring her boobs? She's always on about consideration for others—well, what about Ben and me? We've put up with her barmy job, her bad taste in clothes and her determination to embarrass us all our lives—but turning into a stripper? That's going too far.

She doesn't see it that way, of course.

'I breastfed you,' she said. 'Why should these babies suffer?'

'They won't suffer,' I tell her. 'Bottled milk is just as good.'

'No, it isn't,' she said and went off into a long lecture on the benefits of breastmilk. According to her, it's so brilliant, I'm surprised some enterprising health-food shop doesn't market it. You could have breastmilk yoghurt or cheese! Anyway, Mum was in full rant mode.

'Not enough milk?' she exclaimed. 'Why, that's rarely a problem if you persevere!'

Suzie looked troubled. I was definitely on her side. If her mum was bringing up seven children without breastfeeding them, why couldn't mine manage twins? I was all ready to spring to Suzie's defence, when Gran—trust her—created a diversion.

'You're quite right,' she said, inspecting the milk-jug. 'There's not enough milk. Not if anyone wants another cup of tea. I wonder . . .?' She eyed me hopefully.

'Absolutely, Mother,' said Dad, quick

as a flash. 'I'd certainly like another. Kate, could you . . . ?'

'I'm on my way,' I said, with a grimace. Oh well, crisis averted. For now.

When I returned to the lounge, the conversation had moved on.

'When I was little—when Mum had four of us under five—for a while we had an au pair,' Suzie was saying.

'An au pair!' exclaimed BTM. 'Now there's something we hadn't thought of. I wonder how much they cost . . .'

'Now, Jo . . .' said Dad warningly, but I could see that it was too late. BTM had that look—the one she gets when she thinks she's had a wonderful new idea.

'Oh, they can't cost very much,' said Suzie, 'or we wouldn't have had one. But they do have to have a room of their own.'

'The spare room would be fine,' said BTM delightedly. 'We wouldn't need an au pair for very long. Just while the babies are really little. They can sleep in with us or one could go with Kate and one with Ben.'

'No!' I said.

'No way,' said Ben.

'Why not?' asked Suzie. 'We just have a girls' room and a boys' room. It's not a problem.'

Ben and I glared at her. I wondered if Ben would be quite so keen on her after that.

'Now, Jo,' started Dad. 'We'd have to think about it very carefully. Would it really help, having a stranger in the house?'

'I don't care how strange she is, as long as she can hold a baby and clean the loo!'

'At the same time?' I asked sweetly.

'Are you volunteering?' snapped BTM.

So here we go again. Another can of worms. I can't keep up with this. Blink and your life gets shaken up again. How will we cope with some exotic European swanning around the place? Ben and Chas'll just love that, won't they?

But today had one last surprise in store for us. Ben's cat, Frisk, had come in and taken an instant liking to Suzie.

She does have a very comfortable-looking lap. She fondled her enthusiastically for a while and then said, 'So you're not the only one expecting babies then, Mrs Lofthouse?'

'I'm sorry?' said Mum.

'What?' demanded Ben.

'You mean you didn't know?'

They shook their heads.

'Well, I may be wrong,' said Suzie. 'You could check with my dad. But I'm pretty sure Frisk is pregnant too.'

Honestly! Am I the only one round here who *doesn't* have raging hormones?

5

My Mum and the Kittens

Suzie was right, as it turned out—and we didn't have long to wait. Frisk was very considerate about it. She timed it for a weekend—so Ben could midwife—and camped out in his sock drawer. He was all for moving her but we insisted that he didn't.

'Don't be silly, Ben,' said Mum. 'You mustn't move her if that's where she's decided she needs to be. It would be very disturbing for her.'

'But my socks,' wailed Ben. 'She'll make a mess on my socks!'

I snorted but decided not to say anything. Gran, who had staggered up the stairs to see what was going on, was less tactful. She poked at the mangled heap disdainfully.

'She can hardly make more mess than there is already,' she said. 'And you know where the washing machine is.'

'I suppose,' Ben grumbled, 'that if Mum decides to give birth on my Simpsons duvet you'll all say I've got to let her get on with that too.'

'Now there's a thought,' said BTM, eyeing his bed, 'but actually I was wondering about a water birth.'

'A what?' said Gran.

'Oh, nothing.' BTM pulled a face at us but it was too late.

'Jo, I am neither deaf nor stupid,' said Gran. 'I know perfectly well what you're talking about. Now listen to me. You may look like a whale but kindly remember that you are not one. Water birth, my foot! I've never heard such rubbish!'

At which point, Ben and I collapsed on his Simpsons duvet in helpless giggles.

*   *   *

Gran's insult had no effect, of course. BTM is supremely self-confident. That evening I found her sitting at the kitchen table surrounded by glossy leaflets. I peered over her shoulder.

'What's this?' I demanded, pointing at a photo of what looked like a giant paddling pool. I had my suspicions.

'It's a birthing pool.'

'I thought they had that sort of thing at the hospital.'

BTM looked a bit sheepish. 'I was thinking of having the babies at home, actually.'

I exploded. 'Are you crazy? You were thinking of having the babies here? Think of the . . .' I couldn't think what

63

to say. 'Think of the mess!'

BTM burst out laughing. 'Oh Kate,' she said. 'You're just as bad as Ben. It wouldn't be so funny but neither of you have ever bothered about *mess* before. I'm not thinking about mess myself. I'm thinking about snuggling up in my own bed with my babies afterwards. Just like I did with Ben.'

'But when you had Ben, I wasn't old enough to notice!' I yelled. 'This time we'll have to hang around, listening to you scream!'

BTM could barely control herself. 'You're so funny,' she said. 'You've been watching too much television. I've never got the energy to do much screaming when I'm having a baby. And anyway, the warm water helps with the pain.'

'Oh, fine! So Ben and I will be running up and down with buckets of hot water all night will we?'

'Kate, calm down. The pool would go downstairs. They're too heavy to go in a bedroom. In here would probably be the best place. Nice and cosy and near the taps.'

I looked around the kitchen which was festooned with our usual piles of clutter.

'You . . .' I said firmly, 'have completely lost it.'

'Oh Kate. You're very boring sometimes. I thought you might like to help. See what happens.'

I was speechless. Imagine it! Watching your own mother give birth! Wasn't it bad enough that she wanted to expose her boobs at every opportunity? I'd never be able to look her in the eye again.

'I am going to talk to Dad,' I said, in what I hoped was a very mature voice.

'Really?' said BTM. 'He's in the bath. Starkers, I presume. But perhaps *that* doesn't bother you?'

I felt like hitting her.

*   *   *

Dad wasn't in the bath. He was in the bedroom, drying his hair. Unusually, the door was shut.

'Dad,' I shouted, remembering his complaints last time I'd burst into his

65

room. 'I need to talk to you.'

I heard a groan as he turned off the hairdryer. 'Do you really have to?' he called back.

'Yes.'

He opened the door and let me in.

'Oh well,' he said. 'It was worth a try.'

'What was?'

'Shutting the door, of course. I just thought I'd try for a bit of privacy before I say goodbye to it for another twenty years.'

'Oh,' I said. 'The babies.'

'Yes,' said Dad. 'The babies.'

We looked at one another. Suddenly, it was all too much. I burst into tears.

It all came out. And I mean all of it. All my angst about the babies, the breastfeeding, the au pair, the water birth, the sudden change in Ben—and about Chas and Carly. When I finally ground to a halt, there was silence.

'Sure you've finished?' said Dad.

I nodded and sniffed and scrubbed at my face with the huge hanky he'd handed me.

'Phew!' he said, picking up the

hairdryer again. 'Thought my hair was going to have to dry itself.'

I smiled reluctantly. 'Sorry. But it wouldn't do it any harm. It drives Mum mad the amount of time you spend on it.'

'Quite. Once the babies arrive I'll *have* to leave it to nature—so I'm making the most of my opportunities now. I like drying my hair. It's good therapy. Someone's got to stay sane around here.'

I smiled and waited. Just hearing him fuss about hairdrying made me feel better. I wasn't the only one worrying about what two babies were going to do to us. Shutting my sore eyes, I lay back on the bed and waited for him to finish. I knew he'd be thinking about what I'd said. Dad doesn't rush in headlong with his advice. Not like Mum.

'Now how do they put it in that film *The Life of Brian*? he mused. "Always look on the Bright Side of Life"?'

'I thought you didn't like that film.'

'I don't—but they have a point. You don't have to be quite so gloomy,

Kate. Why worry about tomorrow? Tomorrow will worry about itself. Each day has enough worries of its own.'

I looked at him suspiciously. 'Is that from the Bible?' I demanded. 'That bit about not worrying?'

Dad looked embarrassed. 'Well, sort of.'

'Oh no! Not you as well! It's bad enough Mum spouting bits of Bible all the time! And anyway, you *do* worry!' I retorted. 'That's why you wanted Mum to have all those tests!'

'Did I say I was perfect? Even an old person like me can panic occasionally. But I'm trying not to be *too* pessimistic. It won't help.'

He was right, of course. It didn't help. I sighed.

'You know, I think I'd be managing much better if it wasn't for Chas and Carly. I'd got used to telling Chas everything—but now . . . now . . . well, I don't know . . .'

'But what is all this Chas and Carly stuff? He isn't going out with her, is he? And even if he was, why can't he still be your friend? For goodness' sake, Kate! How old is he? Thirteen? Fourteen? He's hardly likely to marry the girl!'

'But things aren't the same!' I wailed. 'I was perfectly happy. Why couldn't things have just stayed the same?'

Dad shrugged and picked up a band for his ponytail. 'They never do, Kate. Especially relationships. There's another verse I could quote for you.'

I groaned. 'D'you and Mum have a bit of the Bible for absolutely every crisis?'

'Pretty much. Sorry. Does that mean you'd rather I shut up?'

'No. Go on. You might as well tell me.'

' "A friend loves at all times, and a brother is born for adversity." Think about it. And now push off, will you? I came here for some peace.'

I dutifully thought about it in my room for about two minutes and then there was a strangled yelp from next door and Ben burst in.

'Kate,' he gasped. 'Come quickly. Frisk is having her kittens.'

Frisk was very neat about it. You'd think she'd been popping out kittens all her life. We all came in to watch, even Dad in his bathrobe. It was beautiful and Ben didn't say a word about the mess on his socks.

Finally, when Frisk had produced four very healthy-looking babies and they were all snuggled up against her, sucking away, I turned to BTM. I couldn't resist it.

'There,' I said. 'Twice as many babies as you and Frisk didn't need a water birth.'

'No,' agreed BTM. 'The perfect mother. Breastfeeding, of course. And she has *four* babies.'

I glared at BTM. 'Frisk has more teats than you.'

BTM smiled sweetly. 'I only need two,' she said. 'Shall I make a pot of tea?'

*   *   *

It was all rather festive, sitting around drinking tea and eating chocolate biscuits (even Ben allowed himself two) and watching Frisk mother her babies. It made me think life with twins might not be too bad after all. Dad was right. I shouldn't keep worrying about everything.

'I'm going to ring Chas,' I announced. 'He said to let him know when the kittens arrived. Or do you want to do it, Ben?'

Ben looked blank. He was enraptured by the new arrivals. 'What? No, you ring him. I'd better stay with Frisk.' Honestly! Anyone would have thought *he* was the proud father!

I floated downstairs on a cloud of homely bliss. Everything was going to be all right. Birth was beautiful and the twins were going to be adorable, snuggling up with their proud mama. They would gurgle and chortle and, every so often, I would be on hand to cuddle them and give them their bottles and . . . oh, all right, so we hadn't *quite* got that bit sorted yet but there was plenty of time.

I picked up the phone and dialled Chas's number.

Mrs Peterson answered. 'Oh, Kate dear! Yes, I'll just get him. He's across the yard.'

I knew what that meant. Chas has adopted one of the outhouses as his. He can't bear the immaculate tidiness of the house, so he has his own den. It's brilliant. He can play music as loud as he wants, read for hours without anyone interrupting and always seems to have some of the farm's kittens camping out with him. He'll adopt Frisk's if we can't find homes for them. His mother can't bear the den. That's why she politely refers to him being 'across the yard'.

I waited patiently. It would be a while before she was back with Chas. I continued enjoying my dream of bouncing baby bliss.

'Hi Kate,' said Chas, at last. 'What's up?'

Dreamily, I told him the news. He was as excited as we all were.

'Wow, that's great! How many did

she have? Was she OK?'

He wanted all the details, laughed about Ben's socks and we gradually drifted into chatting about this and that. It was just like old times. Dad had been quite right. Why on earth had I been worrying so much?

Just then, I heard someone calling Chas's name in the background. It didn't sound like his mum.

'Oh shoot!' said Chas. 'Sorry, Kate, I'll have to go. I'd completely forgotten what with the kittens and everything. Carly's come over and I've left her on her own. See you, Kate. Bye.'

And that was that. He was gone.

I stood, clutching the phone, my dream in tatters. Carly in Chas's outhouse? Somehow, I'd never imagined him taking anyone there except Ben and me. There was no reason why he shouldn't, of course, but that didn't stop me feeling as if my personal space had been invaded. And how could Carly bear it? Maybe he'd tidied up for her? Somehow that seemed even more of a betrayal. Was he selling out to the tidy people? Going

73

over to his mum's side? I would really lose a friend then. And yet, at the same time, there was this nagging little voice in my head saying, 'He never tidied up for you. He never cared about *you* that much,' which made me wonder exactly what they were up to over there.

I put my head in my hands. What had Dad said? 'A friend loves at all times.' It was easy enough to remember but desperately difficult to do.

6

My Mum and the Minibus

BTM has been in a foul mood for the last few days. Her consultant has told her that there's no way she can have a home birth at her age, especially with twins, and he's not too sure about a water birth either. As if that weren't enough, she and Dad are worrying about money. We're going to have to get another car. BTM's last one ended up in the river and she hasn't replaced it. Dad has one to get to work and, even if he tried to manage on the bus, his car only seats five. And BTM's still sold on this au pair idea. She's worked out that it's by far the cheapest way of getting extra help, which she insists she'll need for a little while at least.

'And it'll be good for Kate and Ben's French,' she insists.

'What if the au pair is Polish?' (That's Ben, of course.)

'She'll be French,' says BTM.

She can be *so* irritating. She hasn't even found a good au pair agency yet.

Anyway, first things first. We have to find a bigger car. There's no way we can afford to buy new and BTM has dismissed all the fancy people carriers anyway.

'Where are you supposed to put your shopping?' she demands regularly. 'And your double buggy?' One foolish salesman suggested she bought a roof-rack. She stared at him as if he was completely deranged.

'What were you thinking I might put up there?' she said witheringly. 'The babies?'

She does have a point though. You can certainly get a lot of people in a people carrier—but nothing much else. So the search is on.

'What about an old double-decker?' she said, the other day. 'We could convert the top and the au pair could have it as a bedroom.'

I know pregnancy is supposed to addle your brain, but really! D'you suppose twice as many babies means twice as much brain damage?

I have just had one of those days. You know—the sort that you'll laugh about eventually but which, right now, is excruciating even to think about. It's Saturday and we all needed to do some shopping, apart from Dad who was working. We got up bright and early so that he could give us a lift into town. The plan was for us to come home on the bus. Normally we all split up and come back when we're ready but Dad was insistent that we stayed with Mum. The babies aren't due for another three months but, boy, is she big. She looks about ready to give birth already. It doesn't help, of course, that she's so short. There's hardly any room between her boobs and her bum on a good day. Anyway, Dad's come over all protective and doesn't like her to go anywhere alone. He seems to think she's in continual danger of total collapse. I thought he was just paranoid—until today.

I should have realized things wouldn't be simple when Mum let out this excited shriek as we whizzed past a car showroom on the edge of town.

'Look at that!' she exclaimed. 'It would be perfect!'

I screwed my head round hard, half-expecting to see the double-decker of her dreams. But instead she was pointing out what looked like a perfectly respectable-looking minibus, sitting on the forecourt.

'Did you see how much it cost?' asked Dad.

'No, but it must have been secondhand or it wouldn't have been outside.'

'I'll try to nip out at lunch time and have a look.'

And that was that. Or so I thought.

By eleven we'd finished our shopping and were having a snack in the bus station café. I was looking forward to cycling over to Chas's house with Vicky and Ben in the afternoon. Carly had a whole day at the dancing school as she was practising for a festival. I should have known better than to relax.

'Look, why don't we go and take a look at that car?' said Mum suddenly. 'It'd save your Dad a job—it's always hard for him to get away from the salon on a Saturday—and anyway, it's me that'll be driving it mostly.'

'Don't you think you've walked far enough today?' said Ben.

'No! It's not far. I'm not an invalid, you know.'

'But we'll never be back in time for the next bus—and I'm meeting Vicky at two.'

'We'll go to McDonald's for once— get some lunch there. Come on—it won't take us long. Then I'll give your dad a ring.'

Ben and I looked at one another. It was pointless trying to argue. When

BTM's set her mind on something, that's it. And McDonald's would be nice. There's always some reason why we don't get there. I should have known better than to hope.

It really wasn't far to the showroom but by the time we arrived, a warm drizzle had set in—the sort that doesn't look particularly wet but soaks you anyway. BTM was still enthusiastic. She lumbered round the minibus, gleefully peering in at the windows and weighing up the luggage space. The price was more than she'd bargained for but she was still hopeful. She was just saying that it looked ideal and maybe she'd let Dad come and look at it anyway when a very respectable man in a suit approached us.

Within moments we'd been ushered into the showroom.

Ben and I exchanged glances. Goodbye McDonald's. Once BTM got talking, there'd never be time to go there. I'd have to grab a biscuit and beg Mrs Charming Peterson for a sandwich. Not that she'd mind—I think it makes her feel good to have to feed neglected children.

'You're new here, aren't you?' said BTM cheerfully to the respectable-looking man. 'What happened to Mr Aston?'

How she knows so many people in this town is beyond me. I mean, as far as I know, she's never even been in that car showroom before. Anyway, I groaned quietly. She'd be after the poor man's life story and we'd be there for hours.

But Mr Respectable was no easy target. He was there to sell cars.

'Mr Aston has retired. Now, you were looking at the Caravelle?'

'Really? Goodness, I didn't realize he was that old! And how long have you been here, then?'

'Since early this year. I thought you might prefer to have a look at the one in the showroom, with the weather being so bad. It's very similar, although it is the newer model, of course.'

'And about twice the price,' muttered Ben.

BTM changed gear. She isn't one to waste her energy. I expect she was like

Violet Elizabeth Bott as a child—you know, from the *William* stories. She could scream and scream until she was sick—but only to get her own way. If Mr Respectable was determined to talk cars, then so be it. I allowed myself a small, silent cheer. We might make it to McDonald's yet.

'I won't be buying new,' she said firmly.

'No matter. Shall I take your coat before you view the interior?' He looked disdainfully at BTM's bright orange cycling cape and I had a sudden protective urge to throttle him with his own silk tie.

We handed over our sopping-wet coats and I, at least, felt a lot better. There was something unnerving about being trapped, soaking wet, in this immaculate, air-conditioned, shiny-floored goldfish bowl with a man who was all permanent press and aftershave. I pushed my damp hair back and prepared to find one of those deeply boring, glossy brochures to while away the time.

That was when the trouble began.

81

Mr Respectable had gone off to talk to a young salesman who seemed to be having a problem with another customer and had left BTM trying out the reclining seats in the back of the Caravelle.

Ben came over. 'You should come and look at this, Kate. It's brilliant. Masses of space and loads of gadgets.'

'Oh yeah? And what about the one outside?'

'We-e-l-l,' said Ben reluctantly. 'More space, less gadgets. It does seat nine, though.'

'Nine! What on earth would we want with nine seats? She's not having quads. I do not want to drive around looking like an episode of "The Waltons"!'

'They didn't have a minibus. And you're not as pretty as Mary Ellen.'

I swiped at him, but he dodged. I suddenly realized that he was getting an awful lot bigger. At this rate, he wasn't going to be my *little* brother for very much longer. Yikes, why did everyone else have to start growing up so fast when I felt (and looked) exactly the same?

At that moment, there was a faint cry from BTM.

'Kate! Ben! I can't get out!'

'Here we go,' said Ben. 'How does she manage it?'

We hurried over. Sure enough, Mum was well and truly stuck. Somehow, the brand-new sliding door on the gleaming minibus had jammed—and BTM was marooned in the back. Ben opened the boot.

'I don't suppose you could climb over the back seats, could you?' he said half-heartedly.

BTM gave him one of her real scorchers. 'Don't be more stupid than you look, please, Ben. Kate, go and get that manager chap.'

But 'that manager chap' had already sensed trouble and was on his way over.

He yanked at the door handle and gave a professional smile.

'They can be a little awkward until you get used to them,' he said smoothly. 'It's just a case of getting the . . . oh!'

We looked at him in disbelief. This was the sort of thing that usually happened to us, not to respectable-looking men in suits. In his hand, he now held part of the handle.

But he rose to the occasion. 'A small technical fault,' he said. 'Easily dealt with. We'll have you out in a moment, madam.'

He pressed a lever and the front seat fell forward. Then, with a flourish, he opened the passenger door.

'If I could ask you to just climb over here . . .' He paused. He obviously hadn't fully taken in BTM's enormous size and limited mobility until that moment.

'He *is* more stupid than he looks,' muttered Ben.

BTM had gone rather pale and was fanning herself with her hand. 'I'm terribly sorry,' she said, 'but I'm feeling rather faint.' There was a pause as she mopped her brow. 'And sick,' she added.

'I'll send for a mechanic,' said Mr Respectable and scurried away.

'A bowl would be more use,' gasped

BTM but he didn't appear to hear her. Probably just as well.

Ben and I stood, rooted to the spot, not knowing what on earth to do.

'I thought you'd stopped feeling sick,' I said stupidly.

'It's the heat,' said BTM. 'And the smell of new plastic. And his rotten aftershave. Now stop standing there gawping and *do* something. *Quickly!*'

I glanced round frantically. Why did places like this never have litter bins? The only container I could see was an ashtray. Then I spotted our shopping bags. Ben, however, had other ideas. To my absolute horror, he dived for one of the huge potted plants and upended it.

'Ben!' I cried. 'No!' And then changed my mind. I mean, which would you rather clean up? Soil on the floor, or sick in a car?

But as Ben shook the pot, nothing happened. The plant was a fake, of course. And the soil was fake too. We'd have to sacrifice a shopping bag.

Just at that moment Mr Respectable came hurrying back, closely followed

85

by a man in overalls and . . . phew! He was carrying a plastic washing-up bowl.

BTM grabbed it gratefully, took a few deep breaths and . . .

'Oh,' she said. 'Thank goodness. I'm beginning to feel a bit better.'

I wasn't though. The door of the showroom had just opened and who should walk in on this scene of chaos but Cute Carly herself.

'Hi Dad,' she said, approaching Mr Respectable with a puzzled look at us all. 'It doesn't look like you're ready for lunch.'

You can guess what BTM did next, can't you?

7

My Mum goes to the Seaside

We bought the minibus—the secondhand one that is. I suppose I'm getting used to it. I mean, all my life BTM's been drawing attention to herself. I guess driving around in a huge red minibus was always on the cards. She adores it, of course. She can only just see over the steering wheel because she has to sit back to leave room for her bump, but she loves being so high up. That's what comes of being so short—you like anything that gives you a feeling of power. Very sad. I thought she'd give it a name—Claribel the Caravelle, or something—but Mum says that's only for anoraks. She can talk!

Anyway, why am I moaning? The summer holidays have begun and I'm determined to take Dad's advice and enjoy them while I can. Why worry about tomorrow? Carly is off the scene for five whole weeks! She's gone to a dancing summer school for a week and then she's jetting off to Florida for a month. Her parents must be loaded. 'Course her mum works too, in a proper job. And Carly's an only child.

Anyway, I'm too happy to be jealous really. Five weeks with only Chas, Ben, Vicky and me. It'll be just like old times. Except for Suzie, of course. And providing the wretched babies don't put in an early appearance. We've been warned to expect anything as twins often do come early. Less than two months to go. Mum's got her hospital bag packed already.

*   *   *

When will I learn not to get overconfident? I forgot, of course, that other people go on holiday too. Chas was away for the first two weeks of the holiday and Vicky has just left for a fortnight in Brittany.

We're not having a holiday this year. We've spent so much on the minibus that we can't even afford to go camping—though we could camp out in one of BTM's maternity dresses. Anyway, apart from the cost, she's nervous about being away from home for too long. Quite right too. I'm writing this at 1 a.m. after one of the longest days of my life. I'm shattered, but too wound up to sleep.

It all started with the weather. Day after day of glorious sunshine—the sort of weather that starts all the grown-ups muttering about hose-pipe bans and stand-pipes. (Question: why is it that everyone wants hot weather until it arrives and then they start complaining? It's the same in winter. Grown-ups go on and on about global warming and never having snow like they did when they were kids but when the first flakes flutter down, do they rush to get out their toboggans? No— they start going on about anti-freeze and slush on the roads and why is Britain never prepared for snow?!)

Anyway, after days of whingeing and wilting like a balloon that's been to too many parties, BTM suddenly started fantasizing about the sea air—how she longed for a sea breeze, and how reviving it would be, just to have one day by the coast. She's chronically short of breath—her lungs are competing for space with two babies—but a quick burst of fresh sea air would make all the difference.

After a full week of moaning and groaning and whingeing and whining, Dad finally gave in. The problem was that he couldn't go. Mum is still working on Sundays and he always works on Saturdays. He doesn't want to take any time off now because he needs to save it up for when the babies arrive. But he didn't want her driving off to the seaside on her own. Given that Britain is an island, we live a depressingly long way from the sea. So we needed another grown-up. The answer was obvious but I wasn't going to say anything.

Chas did though. 'Why don't you ask my mum?' he said, one night over tea.

Really! You can go off some people. Can you imagine Mrs Charming Peterson on a beach? Actually, it's not that difficult. Navy swimsuit with white trim—the hefty sort that turns into shorts at the bottom—and surrounded by everything bar the kitchen sink. I thought when we were packing the car that she'd misunderstood and was planning to go away for a week. Chas and I were staggering in and out of the house for *hours!* Two huge wicker picnic hampers, sunloungers, parasol, at least twenty towels, a whole chemist's shop of sun-lotions, the biggest first aid kit I've ever seen, a rubber dinghy (for Chas I assumed), a set of proper French boules (they weighed a ton), tennis racquets, assorted balls, an array of sunhats and a boomerang. A boomerang? Yes, a boomerang.

'Is it always like this when you go to the seaside?' I asked Chas.

He looked at the heap critically. 'No,' he said. 'We haven't got the wine chiller today.'

I gazed at our small pile of tatty buckets and spades and threadbare beach towels and sighed.

We set off bright and early (I already felt as if I'd done a full day's work), in the Petersons' Land Rover. BTM had thrown a slight tantrum over that—she wanted to take her red minibus. But Dad put his foot down.

'Don't be ridiculous. There's no point in you driving if you don't have to. If I hear another word, you won't go.'

She sulked but shut up. Dad doesn't often throw his weight about (let's face it, she weighs more than him) but when

91

he does, she takes notice. And she'd already won one victory—we were taking Gran.

Yes, can you believe it? You'd have thought that it was enough to take one deranged semi-invalid to the seaside, but no, we had to take two. Mum insisted that we couldn't possibly have a day out without letting Gran escape from her nursing home. Dad wasn't happy, despite all Mum's attempts to lay on the guilt ('Your own mother! How can you be so mean?') but Mrs Charming Peterson was prepared to cope—even though Gran has a slight bladder problem. Perhaps *that's* why she was taking twenty towels!

All went well on the journey there. We sang, played games, listened to tapes and ate breakfast from the first of the picnic hampers—croissants, which were still warm because Mrs Peterson had wrapped them in about a dozen large napkins. (Does she have shares in a laundry?) I'd thought Ben might sulk because we weren't taking Suzie but he didn't seem to give her a thought. He might think they're like

Chas and me but really he has no idea.

There were no problems with the traffic and we found our secret free parking space, just two minutes' walk from our favourite beach. It took us a mere half-hour to unpack!

It was only as I watched Mrs Peterson wriggle neatly out of her smart walking shorts that I had a sudden ghastly thought. What on earth was BTM going to wear? Surely she wasn't going to reveal the full horror of her shape to the world at large?

She saw my appalled face and grinned. 'It's all right, Kate. I haven't bought a maternity swimsuit. I wouldn't fit, even in one of them. I'll stay as I am.'

It could have been worse—she was in her favourite Fat Willy's Surf Shack T-shirt, a huge hat and baggy trousers. (We were spared the sight of her new varicose veins—ugh!)

'Aah, bliss!' she declared, settling herself back on one of the Petersons' sunloungers (which, surprisingly, didn't collapse). '*I am* glad we came.'

So was I, actually. The weather was

fantastic and we'd set off so early that the beach still wasn't crowded. Chas, Ben and I made the most of the space and played tennis and boules and rounders until we were too hot to carry on. Chas and Ben had a lovely time showing off their hairless chests.

'Go and have a swim,' said BTM. 'I'm off to find some ice creams. And don't ask me to get you a Feast, Ben, because I won't.'

Ben grinned. He hasn't been allowed a Feast ever since he had one at the cinema and threw it up again an hour or so later, all over someone else. The someone else deserved it but still . . .

'How about a Double Magnum?' he suggested cheekily.

'No way. Only I get one of them. Half for each baby.'

'Oh, go on Mum!' Ben pleaded.

'I'll think about it. No, don't argue.'

With that, she heaved herself off her sunlounger and staggered off along the beach.

I watched her fondly. The sun and the fun were making me mellow. And from the back, you could hardly tell she was pregnant. At least while she was obsessed with babies, she hadn't the energy for any other daft projects.

Forty minutes later, having splashed and shrieked till we were hoarse and feeling distinctly peckish, we trailed back to the holiday village which Mrs Charming Peterson had set up on the sand. Gran was snoring peacefully in a deckchair—she had turned her nose up at the new-fangled sunloungers—and Mrs Charming was snoozing too. But where was BTM? She should have been back long ago.

'Uh-oh,' said Ben. 'Are you thinking what I'm thinking?'

'You don't think . . .' I started. I was beginning to panic already.

'No, I don't think she's giving birth on a sanddune. I think she's probably met a long-lost friend and is having a natter—and she won't remember us until our ice creams melt all over her bump. But we'd better go and look.'

'Shall I . . .?' Chas was about to prod his mum.

'NO!' said Ben and I together. The thought of Mrs Charming Peterson going into Mrs Fix-it mode was too much.

Chas looked uncertain.

'There's no point in worrying her yet,' I said soothingly. 'It's probably nothing—but you'd better stay here in case she wakes up and is worried about where we are.'

It was only a few minutes' walk to the ice cream kiosk and it didn't take us long to scour that part of the beach. No sign of BTM—and she was hard to miss.

'Now what?' said Ben.

'I dunno,' I said uneasily. 'I haven't heard any ambulance sirens . . .'

'Don't be silly. I bet she's gone to the next kiosk. This one doesn't do Double Magnums.'

'Are you serious?'

'Of course,' said Ben. 'We chocoholics understand each other.'

'But I can't even see the next kiosk!'

'That wouldn't bother BTM.'

Off we trudged. I was beginning to fantasize about an ice-cool Calippo.

It was when we were almost at the second kiosk that we finally found

BTM. I was down by the shoreline, thinking she might have paddled along in the shallows to keep cool, when I heard a shout from Ben who had been searching near the prom.

All I could see was a huge pile of sand—someone had been very busy—but sure enough once I got closer, I spotted my accident-prone mother marooned behind it.

'Don't ask silly questions,' she gasped before I had chance to get started. 'I slipped. It's hard to see where you're putting your feet with a bump this size and six ice creams. You're very lucky I'm not in the hospital.'

I know it was wicked but all I could think about was getting BTM back to the kiosk as soon as possible. I could see two cones upended and melting in the sand and felt saliva gathering in my mouth.

'The trouble is,' BTM explained, 'that I can't get a grip in this sand and I'm all off-balance. But it'll be easier now you're here and without the ice creams.'

'What's happened to the rest of them?' I asked suspiciously.

BTM looked at me and blushed.

'I ate them.'

'What, *all* of them?'

'Well, there was no point in letting them go to waste.'

'What, including my Double Magnum?' Ben looked as if someone had just strangled Frisk's kittens.

BTM looked sheepish. 'And mine,' she admitted. 'What could I do?'

'You deserve to be sick,' I said.

'Please! Don't! Just help me up.'

'Couldn't you have shouted for help?' I demanded. 'Or prayed for someone to come and rescue you?'

BTM cleared her throat and looked out to sea.

Actually,' she said, 'I was having quite a nice time with the ice creams.'

Unfortunately, helping her up proved to be more difficult than she anticipated. It must have been something to do with her centre of gravity (abnormal at the best of times) and the fact that the sand kept slipping away beneath her feet. It didn't matter how hard we pulled, we just couldn't get her up.

'Suppose I pushed and you pulled?' said Ben.

I shook my head. 'I'd be worried about her falling forwards and flattening the babies.'

'Not to mention you!'

'Stop talking as if I'm not here,' complained BTM. 'We'll just have to get someone to help.'

Easier said than done. I didn't like to go and disturb any of the dozing sunbathers, so I accosted the first person walking towards us, a nice mumsy-looking lady. Do you find that years of non-stop Stranger Danger makes you incredibly wary of approaching anyone who isn't wearing a uniform, or is female and pushing a double-buggy?

'I'm sorry—I'm afraid I've got my hands full at the moment,' she said. She had—four 99s. I eyed them enviously, then tried again.

This time I approached two teenage boys with bronzed chests to die for.

'Excuse me . . .' I started but they

didn't even pause—just exchanged glances and walked on.

' 'Fraid they didn't fancy you, Kate,' said Ben, so I thumped him.

'You try then, smarty-pants,' I snapped.

The next person was a furious woman with a wailing toddler.

'Hopeless,' I said. 'Look, how about him?'

Approaching us jauntily was a huge man absolutely covered in tattoos. I've just read this book by Jacqueline Wilson called *The Illustrated Mum.* Well, this was the illustrated beach-bum. I wouldn't have fancied meeting him on a dark night. Thick-set, shaved head, heavy jaw, lots of bulging muscles. Definitely Neanderthal.

'Perfect,' said Ben. 'Excuse me.'

He stopped. 'Wotcha, mate.'

Within seconds he'd got the picture, thrust his ice cream into my hand, (how I didn't eat it, I don't know) and hauled BTM to her feet.

'Thank you very much indeed,' she said, dusting herself down and looking flustered. Then . . .

'Just a minute . . .' Recognition was

dawning in her eyes. I couldn't believe it. Does she know everyone on this entire planet?

'Jo!' said Mr Neanderthal. 'Jo Lofthouse!'

'Ted! It is Ted, isn't it?'

Mum gave us a beaming grin. 'We worked together on a summer playscheme one year.'

Oh great! She'd be standing there chatting for hours. And what about our ice creams?

'Would you like this back now?' I said, holding out Ted's cone as a hint.

'Thanks, luv,' said Ted and took it. That was when I noticed the tattoos across his knuckles. I peered surreptitiously at his other hand.

'GOD LOVES U2,' I read. One letter on each knuckle.

God loves U2? Well, I'm sure he does—they're a great band—but it seemed a funny thing to have tattooed on your fingers.

Ted caught my puzzled expression and grinned. 'Had it done years ago, luv,' he said. 'Before *they'd* even been thought of. I meant "God loves *you too!*" '

Well, what d'you know? A whole beach full of sun-worshippers and we have to find another signed-up member of the God squad.

8

My Mum and the Train

We did get our ice creams in the end and the rest of the day passed off peacefully. Mum and Ted had a great time catching up on the last fifteen years—it turned out that he was working in the area and had an afternoon off. It was when home time came that the trouble really started.

The car wouldn't start. Ted, who dragged up most of our stuff from the beach, helped us try to jump-start it— but it was no good. It was completely dead. We all peered hopefully under the bonnet but only because we felt we ought to. None of us knew the first thing about cars. I'd expected Ted to immediately cry, 'Ah, of course, it's the carburettor!' or some other bit of meaningless technospeak but he just shook his head despondently. He isn't some sort of mechanic as I'd assumed but a *nurse*—which just shows you shouldn't judge by appearances.

'So what shall we do?' I demanded impatiently. I was tired and sweaty and couldn't wait to get home and into the shower.

'Well, I could get some of you down to the station,' said Ted. 'Jo looks shattered—and, if you're lucky, you'll get a through train.'

'Better start praying!' said Mum.

She did look shattered. I thought of suggesting that we all prayed that the car miraculously started but decided that was too silly. I regretted it later.

Anyway, we quickly sorted ourselves out. Mrs Peterson would wait for the recovery service and the rest of us would catch the train. It would take Ted two trips to the station but he didn't mind. His car was only up the road, so we left Mum and Gran resting in the Land Rover and set off.

As soon as we got to the station, we checked the timetable.

'Crikey!' said Chas. 'The last through train is in half an hour. D'you think we can make it?'

'No probs,' said Ted. 'Get in the queue for the tickets. I'd give you the dosh but I haven't got enough.'

Trying to stay calm while we waited was impossible. Chas kept saying that it didn't really matter—there was always another train—but we all knew that meant a change and endless hanging around. It just didn't bear thinking about, especially with Gran in tow.

'I wish we could have left Gran with your mum,' said Ben to Chas.

'Oh shut up!' I snapped. 'How is whingeing going to help? You know perfectly well she's too confused these days to be left with someone she doesn't know very well.'

'Mum left her when she went to get the ice creams!'

'That was only supposed to be for a few minutes!'

It was horrible. We were all tired, irritable and too stressed out to be nice to each other.

At long last, with only minutes to go, we spotted Mum. She was doing her best to run and Ted was dragging Gran along after her. Mum panted up to the ticket kiosk where we had been taking it in turns to guard a place in the queue, showered us all with old receipts and tissues as she fumbled for her cards, and then, clutching her bump protectively, hobbled after us. Ben ran ahead to try to make the train wait. Chas and I grabbed Mum by the elbows and hauled her along while Ted struggled with Gran.

'Don't hurry me, young man,' I could hear her complaining. 'I'm perfectly capable of managing by myself.'

Fortunately, Ben managed to sweet-talk the guard into hanging on for a few moments and we bundled Mum and Gran onto the train. They both looked dreadful. Ted shouted a breathless goodbye and the train started moving.

'Oh crikey!' said Chas. 'What about seats?'

This is the sort of situation where

BTM normally takes charge. One steely look round and she has men in suits wilting. Today, she leaned against the loo door and panted.

'I'm not sure I can get through there,' she said, waving a limp hand at the automatic door.

' 'Course you can,' I said firmly. 'Just wait here while we find some seats.'

I stalked into the crowded carriage and raised my voice.

'Excuse me,' I said. 'Is there anyone here who could give up their seat for a pregnant lady and a ninety-year-old granny, please?'

Gran is only in her eighties actually but she looked at least a hundred just then. I thought God would forgive me a little exaggeration; it was all in a good cause.

Everyone glanced at each other and then looked away quickly. You know what the British are like. Good at queuing and singing football songs together but ask them to stand out in a crowd and you'd think you'd requested a live brain transplant.

'What? Nobody?' I said, in ringing

tones. I'm in training to become a tour guide. I could see Chas and Ben cringing in the corridor, but I didn't care.

In the end, a young couple whose quiet snog I'd rudely interrupted stood up and shuffled along the gangway. 'We'll be OK out there,' said the bloke. I was sure they would be. More privacy, actually.

Ever tried manoeuvring a heavily pregnant woman through an overcrowded train? It took the next five minutes to get BTM into the carriage. In the end, however, both she and Gran were safely seated, while Chas, Ben and I perched on armrests.

'Wow, Kate!' said Chas, giving me a look of blatant admiration. 'That was fantastic!'

I forgave him everything, including the evening in his den with Cute Carly.

'Almost as good as your mum,' he added.

I imagined chewing him into small pieces and spitting them deliberately out of the train window. Then I would start on Carly.

It was incredibly hot in the carriage. Air-conditioning is all very well but give me a window you can open, any day. Right that minute I felt like hanging my head out like an over-heated dog. I was just wondering whether it was worth struggling to the buffet to see if they had any chilled drinks when BTM clutched her bump and sucked in her breath sharply.

'Ouch!' she said.

'You OK?' asked Ben anxiously.

She smiled bravely. 'I think I've rearranged the babies with all that running. They're just sorting themselves out.'

I wasn't convinced. This was no time to disappear in search of drinks. I watched her like a hawk.

'Stop staring at me, Kate,' she complained. 'I'm fine. Just need a few minutes to . . . oof!'

Our eyes locked. I detected the slightest hint of panic. Oh no, I thought. Here comes trouble. Time to start praying.

'What is it, Mum?' said Ben anxiously. 'Are you sure you're all right?'

'Stop fussing, Ben. I'm fine. They'll settle down in a minute. I just need to sit quietly for a minute. Probably a bit of indigestion too. Shouldn't have eaten all that ice cream. I . . . aargh!' This time several people nearby looked up, startled, including Gran, who had been dozing off.

Ben promptly panicked. 'You're having contractions, aren't you Mum? All that running—it's started the babies coming!'

Chas had been peering over someone's shoulder, trying to read their newspaper. 'What did you say?' he interrupted. 'The babies are coming?'

Gran was still half-asleep but she had heard enough. Before any of us could stop her, she'd launched herself out of her seat and reached the emergency alarm.

'NO!' we all shrieked—but it was too late. Immediately, the train gave a great shudder—and all hell was let loose. Gran was thrown against the table so hard that her false teeth shot out across the carriage and Ben, who had tried to grab her, fell flat on his face. Fine—except that a smartly dressed young business woman was approaching with a coffee from the buffet, so she went flying over Ben's legs and the drink showered a man reading *The Sun.*

I think I heard every swear word known to man in the ensuing minutes —and then some.

'Oh sh . . .!' said BTM. 'And I'm sure I'm going to be all right.'

'Don't be silly, dear,' said Gran, who had popped her teeth back in which Chas had rather queasily retrieved. 'Of course you won't be here all night. Not now I've stopped the train.'

'*She* won't be,' snapped a man across the gangway, 'but the rest of us b . . . well will!'

'Oh shut up!' retorted Ben, who had scrambled to his feet. 'Can't you see she's having a baby?'

'Two!' cried Gran triumphantly. 'She's having twins!'

At which point the whole carriage erupted, all over again.

To be fair, after that, things were sorted out pretty quickly. The business woman was charm itself and the guard, who appeared within moments, soon had the measure of the situation. An appeal for a doctor was made, miraculously one appeared, and that good old wartime spirit that the Brits do so well (not to mention queueing and singing football songs) soon filled the carriage. Everyone was having such a good time complaining about the heat and telling each other about the last time they were stuck in a traffic jam/lift/ferris wheel/hi-jack that there was quite an air of disappointment when the train finally got moving.

None of this *joie de vivre* touched me. I was panicking. I didn't like the plan. The doctor wanted Mum to be ambulanced to hospital at the next station.

'I'm sure everything will be fine,' she said reassuringly, 'but better safe than sorry. You really don't want to have the babies here.'

So far so good. But what about Gran? How could we get her home?

Mum wasn't happy for us to be left to look after Gran on the train, so Chas and Ben were told to stay put and ring Chas's dad when they arrived while I— I had to go to the hospital with BTM and Gran! Dad would have to drive down to collect us. It was going to take hours, even though we phoned Dad and he was setting out immediately.

'What else do you suggest?' demanded BTM, seeing my appalled face. 'There's no point in you all coming to the hospital. Would you prefer me to leave Gran on the train with you?'

I bit my lip. No, she was right. That would be worse. Gran had dozed off again after all the excitement, but there was never any knowing what she might do next. At least in a hospital there was a chance there'd be someone who knew how to handle batty old ladies.

I sneaked out of the carriage to lick my wounds. I was very close to crying and didn't want to disgrace myself in front of a whole carriage full of people. Although it says you shouldn't, I pulled down the window in the door and stuck my head out. The wind rushing past cooled my scarlet face.

'Shove up a bit, can't you?' said Chas and squeezed his shoulders in beside mine.

I should have been too fed up and tired to care but I couldn't help noticing the pressure of his arm against mine. The temptation to turn round and cry on his shoulder was almost irresistible.

'The end of a perfect day, huh?'

'Oh shut up,' I said. 'It isn't funny.'

'Come on, Kate! Lighten up! It's not that bad. You'll be home before midnight if you're lucky. And I'm sure your mum'll be fine. She thinks she will be.'

'Yes, but what about me?' Even as I said it, I could have cut out my tongue. There I was again, moaning on about *me*. Was it surprising that Chas got fed up? But I was too tired and upset to control myself. 'How on earth am I going to cope with Gran? What if she goes and wees all over the place?'

'Kate, you're going to a hospital! They deal with things like that all the

113

time! And, anyway, I thought all that had been sorted out?'

'Oh, I know, I know, I'm just panicking—I'm tired and I want to go home. I'm sorry.'

Chas gave me an encouraging smile. 'You'll be fine, Kate. Look how you got those seats for your mum and your gran. Just like your mum before she got pregnant. You'll cope.'

I wasn't angry this time—just depressed. So I was a clone of BTM, was I? Loud-mouthed, bossy and bonkers. Great. You win, Cute Carly.

*   *   *

The drive to the hospital seemed to take for ever. Everyone always likes the idea of a trip in an ambulance—all sirens and flashing lights—but of course, when you need one, you're too ill to notice. In this case, the ambulance barely got above twenty miles per hour as the paramedics were anxious to keep Mum as still as possible. They were brilliant, of course. One of them managed to keep Gran chatting all the way there and still watched Mum like a hawk.

It was when we got to Accident and Emergency that the trouble began again. Mum was whisked off on a stretcher and I parked Gran in the waiting area while I went to the loo. I was tired, I was stupid, I should never have taken my eyes off her. She seemed exhausted after all the excitement and it never entered my head that she wouldn't stay where I put her. I washed my face, combed my hair and gulped down some water so was feeling a hundred times better—until I saw the empty chair. At first, I thought I'd made a mistake or that Gran had simply changed her seat. Then I checked the loos. Then I panicked.

'I've lost my Gran,' I shrieked at the receptionist.

She looked a little surprised. I must have seemed a big girl to need a Gran to look after me.

'Well, just sit tight, dear, and I'm sure she'll find you. You'll be perfectly safe here.'

'No, no,' I wailed. 'It's me that's

supposed to be looking after *her* and she's gone and wandered off. She gets very confused, you ...'

'Excuse me, dear—I'll just take this call ...'

'But ...' How could I make the silly woman understand? Gran could be anywhere. Interrupting operations, falling down stairs, walking under ambulances ...

'Oh forget it,' I snapped. 'I'll look myself ...'

OK, it was stupid. I know, I know, I should have stayed where I was. But, as I said, I panicked.

I hurried outside and scoured the car park. Nothing. Back into the waiting room. No. Loos again. No Gran. I dashed through the nearest swing-doors and set out. Down corridors. Up endless flights of stairs. Peering through glass doors. Checking waiting areas. On and on, all at a mad dash, getting hotter and hotter, gasping for another drink and feeling as though my legs would give way. Result? Nothing. It was only when I glanced at a clock and saw that I must have been gone for nearly a whole hour that I realized how stupid I was being. I collapsed on the nearest chair and put my head in my hands. What on earth was I going to do? I needed a quick way back to Accident and Emergency and I didn't know where to start.

Now there's one thing about God. It doesn't matter how fed up you are with him and how little you think you believe in him, there's always the possibility that he's out there listening. So I did the first sensible thing I'd done since getting those seats for Mum and Gran. I prayed. I prayed that Gran would be safe and that I would find her quickly.

There was a tap on my shoulder.

'Kate?' said a voice I vaguely recognized. 'Kate? What the blazes are you doing 'ere?'

I looked up and couldn't believe my eyes. A miracle! Ted! Of course! He was a nurse, wasn't he? And this was his hospital! Well, why not? It wasn't as if we'd travelled very far before Gran had set off the alarm.

After that, it was easy. Ted escorted

me back to A&E, where Gran was sitting dozing in a chair, an empty plastic cup by her side. She'd been off to find a drinks machine. I avoided thinking about her staggering along with a cup of scalding tea—the worst obviously hadn't happened. Ted got a drink and biscuits for me, and let me cry on his shoulder—which was a lot bigger and more comforting than Chas's would have been. Then—second miracle of the evening—Dad came marching in, having driven flat out and reached us in an hour and forty minutes.

And finally—miracle number three—BTM came strolling out through some double doors, having been released to go home and take it easy. There had been no sign of any more contractions and the babies had settled down.

'I said I'd be all right,' she complained as she sorted out her seat belt.

'And I said you shouldn't take my mother,' grumbled Dad.

I curled up on the back seat and

thought about all that had happened. Maybe God was keeping an eye on me, after all. Maybe there was a good reason for the twins coming. Maybe. I would wait to be convinced.

9

My Mum Makes a Mistake

September has arrived and so has Carly, worse luck. I had one whole week kicking around with Chas before Vicky came home and then another two with them both. We've seen a lot of Suzie too and she's fitted in brilliantly. Why can't Carly be like her? As soon as she got back, I mentioned it to Vicky. She gave me a pitying look.

'Kate, sometimes I think you're completely dense. What does it matter what Carly's like? Chas fancies her, therefore you hate her.'

'That's not true!' I retorted. 'I wouldn't mind if he fancied someone decent . . .'

'Like me? Or Suzie? Dream on! You couldn't bear it! As far as you're concerned, Chas is yours and God help any poor girl who lays a finger on him.'

'But I . . .' I stopped. I was thinking about it. What if Chas *did* suddenly start showing as much interest in Vicky as he did in Carly? I suddenly felt very uncomfortable. No—surely not? It was just that Carly was such a prat—always so dainty and concerned about how she looked.

'You see!' said Vicky triumphantly. 'You can't answer that! What I can't understand is why you don't do something about it. If you just made a bit of an effort, Chas would wilt. It's not as if you're bad-looking. And he obviously really likes you. I bet that's the reason he still hasn't asked Carly out—he's confused, poor thing.'

'But . . .'

'Oh, never mind, Kate. Forget I said anything. But I bet I'm right.'

How can I forget? I'm frantic. What's stopping me then? Apart from the small matter of not knowing quite what Vicky means. What am I supposed to do? Pin Chas down and snog him?

More importantly though, I'm not sure I want to. I went through all this last year and thought I'd got it sorted. If Chas and I go out together and then finish, that's it. End of friendship. It happens all the time. I can't risk that. Anyway, I think Vicky's wrong. I mean, how does Chas see me? Just like BTM! That's what he said anyway! And he certainly doesn't fancy her! I reckon I'm like the sister he's never had.

*   *   *

Well, whatever I might have done, it's too late now. Disaster! Everything's happened at once. Today was our first day back at school—and Ben's first at the comprehensive. He seemed pretty cool about the whole thing—apart from spending even more hours than usual in front of the mirror this morning.

'Come on, Ben,' I yelled, hammering on the bathroom door. 'You've got one girlfriend. How many more do you want?'

'That's not the point,' he growled, letting me in. 'First impressions count.'

I wagged my finger at him. 'Don't let BTM hear you say that,' I said. 'Your inner beauty is more important, remember.'

He looked pained. 'My inner beauty is perfect,' he said. 'I haven't eaten any junk food for months.'

I sighed. 'That's not what I meant. Now get out of my way, will you?'

All the same, he did look pretty good. He's grown quite a bit and looks really solid. I glanced at my own reflection and sighed. I looked OK— but I've looked OK since I was eleven. I fancied a change. I held up my long hair experimentally.

'Reckon I should have it cut?' I asked Ben.

'No way,' he said. 'It's gorgeous.'

'What?' I looked at him as if he'd sprouted three heads. I'm not used to compliments from Ben.

'Well, you did ask,' he said, shuffling about uncomfortably. 'Thought you ought to know.'

'Well, thank you,' I said and preened myself slightly.

'Don't let it go to your head though,' he added. 'You could still do with a bit less bum and bigger boobs.'

I threw a wet sponge in his face. So there you have it—yet another bloke who thinks I'm turning into my mum. It wasn't a good start to the day.

It got worse. Chas has been spending a lot of time with Carly since she got home. Well, it was understandable as he'd hardly seen her all summer. But somehow I hadn't expected it to make much difference to us—we'd been getting on so well while Carly was away that I'd convinced myself we were best friends again. And then, suddenly, there I was alone in my new tutor room and Chas nowhere in sight. I decided I'd catch up with him at break but couldn't find him anywhere. I finally ran him to ground at lunch time when I checked up on how Ben was getting along—Chas was doing exactly the same thing, with Carly in tow. It was awful. Vicky was sympathetic but had a distinct air of 'I-told-you-so' about her.

Worse still, I saw a couple of bitchy girls who I'd had trouble with in the past nudging each other and talking behind their hands about me.

'Has Charlie-boy finally dumped you, Katie?' called out one.

'What's it to you if he has?' I retorted but it didn't make me feel any better.

By the end of school, I was in a really foul mood. I stomped outside, determined to get away before Chas had a chance to catch me—supposing he was even considering it. My heart sank even further when, staggering towards me, I saw BTM. She's well known around school—she's forever doing assemblies or helping out with RE or acting as a kind of unpaid school counsellor—but, of course, no one had seen her for six weeks and she'd grown quite a lot in that time. I think the polite word is 'bloomed' but 'exploded' is nearer the mark. With less than a month to go, she was having great difficulty finding any clothes that would fit. Today she was sporting a huge pair of Ali Baba trousers and an enormous black shawl. She looked like an extra for a Clint Eastwood western. I could see everyone staring as she waddled over to meet me. What on earth was she doing here? Surely she hadn't come to check that Ben was OK? He would die!

'Kate!' she gasped. 'A slight crisis. I don't know how I've managed this but I've got the wrong date for the au pair arriving. I thought it was tomorrow and it's today. She's just called from Victoria Coach Station wondering why no one's there to meet her. And she sounded terribly gruff—like she'd got a bad sore throat. I can't possibly expect her to find her own way from London.'

'So?' I said. 'Why are you here?'

'Because I'm going to have to drive down and get her—as soon as possible. Your dad can't leave the salon—so he wants you to go with me, in case there's a problem. He went ballistic but I've got to go.'

'I don't believe it!' I said. I deliberately hadn't been thinking about the au pair. Dad's 'why worry about tomorrow?' philosophy had been coming in very handy—but suddenly tomorrow had become today.

'Well, start believing it! Go and find Ben for me and then we'll go—unless he wants to go home with Chas. I don't suppose his mum will mind.'

'Chas might though,' I muttered.

'Why?'

'Oh, it doesn't matter.'

'Well, stop being so grouchy and go and find him! I'll wait in the car.'

Well! The last thing I fancied after the miserable day I'd had was a trip to London in the rush hour. And I was in no mood to be friendly and welcoming to an au pair. I'd been plotting a nice, hot bubble bath and slobbing out in front of the TV—my last chance before all the homework started mounting up. So I was in a truly disgusting mood when I ran into Chas.

'Kate!' he said breathlessly. 'I was trying to catch you before you went home.'

'Really?' I snapped. 'I can't think why. You seem to have been avoiding me all day. Anyway, I can't stop. I've got to find Ben and see if he wants to go home with you or come up to London to collect our au pair.'

'What? The au pair? Now?'

'Yes. Typical, isn't it? Mum's so brain-dead at the moment that she got the wrong day. Knowing our luck, we'll probably end up at the wrong coach station too! I'm fed up with the whole business and the au pair hasn't even got here yet, let alone the wretched babies.'

'Oh Kate! You're always whingeing! The au pair might be really nice!'

'Yeah? Well, you would think that, wouldn't you? You're just like Ben and all the other boys I know. Only interested in one thing. And I always thought you were different.'

Chas's cheeks turned a dull red. I knew I'd gone too far. Guiltily, I recalled one of Mum's favourite Bible verses—'No man can tame the tongue. It is a restless evil, full of deadly poison.' Well, too right. Chas looked as if he'd swallowed arsenic.

'There's something I've been meaning to tell you for a few days, Kate Lofthouse,' he almost spat, 'but it doesn't sound like you'd want to know—so I won't bother.' Then he turned on his heel and stalked away.

'What's up with you, then?' said Ben, when I finally found him. 'You look sick as a parrot.'

I told him.

'Oh sh . . . !' he said.

'The au pair or Chas?' I asked.

'Both.'

I don't suppose Chas made his next move deliberately. He's not malicious. He wouldn't plan something to hurt me. It just happened. Ben tried to protect me. We were walking past the bike racks when he suddenly grabbed my arm.

'Hey, look Kate! There's a fox over there—look, over on the field. Fancy that—in broad daylight!'

I think it was the 'fancy that' which gave him away. Just a bit too staged. I didn't look at the field, I looked at the bike racks. Silly me. There was Chas, kissing Cute Carly. In broad daylight. Fancy that.

I sat in the back seat of the car and tears poured silently down my cheeks. I

128

was never more glad that BTM had become so enormous. She can barely lean forward to check for traffic at junctions, let alone turn round and look at me. Ben kept stroking my hand helplessly. He even managed to find two squashed bits of chocolate to hand to me. A friend loves at all times, huh? Sorry. Impossible. But Ben's pretty good at the 'brother born for adversity' bit.

By the time we hit the M25, I had mopped myself up. After all, I didn't want to look a complete wreck, the first time I met the exotic European. Then I spent some time analysing why I was so upset. It's obvious really. You can't be best friends with someone who's got a girlfriend. The girlfriend gets in the way. Vicky's quite right. I'd be just as mad if it were her or Suzie. So that's it. I can't pretend Chas is my most special friend any more; he's made that very clear. No one will believe me, of course, but they can think what they like. I know the truth. I just wish . . . well, I just wish I hadn't been so horrible to him. It's not exactly how I'd want to end a beautiful friendship. I do wish I could learn to control my big mouth.

Anyway, the day wasn't over yet. There was another shock in store.

'How are we going to recognize the au pair?' asked Ben, as we juddered our way through the rush-hour traffic.

'I've brought the photo,' said Mum, 'and she said in her letter she'd be wearing a black body-warmer and grey trousers. Anyway, she shouldn't have much trouble spotting *me*. Have a look at the photo if you want—it's in my bag.'

We'd seen the photo before when it came with the agency's recommendation but neither of us had taken much notice. We'd been too busy enjoying the summer to bother. Now, however, I was intrigued. It wasn't a great photo though.

'She looks a bit butch,' said Ben doubtfully.

Mum laughed. 'All the better for hoicking babies about,' she said.

I studied the picture. Shoulder length dark hair with a centre parting, smiley eyes and a firm chin. She did look like a strapping girl—the sort you might imagine mucking out a farmyard in wellies.

'She looks fine,' I pronounced. 'Nice and sensible.'

'Not what I imagined French girls to be like,' said Ben morosely.

'Serves you right for being racist,' I said.

'It's not racist. I just thought she'd be more . . .'

'Sexy?' I suggested.

'Oh shut up,' said Ben.

*   *   *

Victoria Coach Station at 5.30 p.m. was like the Tower of Babel. Everyone in a hurry and spouting a different language. I looked on in despair. How on earth were we to find someone in a black body-warmer and grey trousers in all that? (Question: why does *everyone* in London seem to wear black or grey?)

'Where did she say she would be?' I demanded.

BTM looked twitchy. 'I haven't been here for years,' she said, 'so I said by the arrivals board. I'm not even sure there is one.'

'Bound to be,' said Ben. 'Come on.'

But Mum looked exhausted. 'Sorry you two—I'll have to sit down for a minute—and I don't like the idea of pushing my way through this lot.'

Neither did I and I haven't got a huge bump to protect.

'OK,' I said. 'Let's find a seat.'

Fortunately, BTM is so vast now, that as soon as we approached a bench, someone leapt up to make space. I was very aware of all the curious glances.

'I'm beginning to understand how it must feel to be in a wheelchair or have a terrible deformity,' said Mum. 'Everywhere I go, there're people trying not to stare. A total stranger stopped me in the street the other day and asked me if I was having triplets.'

'What did you say?'

'I said, "Yes—and all by different men."' She laughed briefly. 'I know I shouldn't have, but honestly!'

I smiled and felt ashamed of myself.

Chas was so right. Why *did* I have to go on whingeing? The last few weeks must have been terrible for Mum.

Ben had been scouring the crowds.

'Look,' he said. 'Over there. There's someone in a black body-warmer and grey trousers. And the hair's right.'

I followed his gaze. Sure enough, standing under the arrivals board with a pile of luggage and a rather dejected air, was someone who matched our photo surprisingly well.

'Mum, did the au pair say anything about how tall she was?'

'Oh yes—I'd forgotten. She said she was very tall.'

'And does she play a musical instrument?'

'Oh goodness, yes—now what was it? A cello, I think.'

'Give us the photo—quick!'

'Why? What's the problem?' said Mum, groping in her bag.

Ben and I studied the photo hard. Our eyes met. Ben nodded. 'Definitely,' he said.

'What's up?' said Mum. 'Have you spotted her?'

'Oh yes,' I said. 'We've spotted her. Or rather we've spotted *him*.'

10

My Mum Goes Out to Lunch

'What?' shouted Dad, through the bathroom door. 'What did you say? I'm in the shower!'

'I *said* the au pair is a bloke.'

'That's what I thought you said. So? What's the problem?'

'But we were expecting a girl! I don't want three blokes leaving their hair in the bath and peeing on the bathroom floor!'

'What d'you mean—three? I'm innocent.'

'No, you're not. You're worse than Ben. And *you* leave your whiskers in the sink too. Another bloke'll make more work, not less!'

'Just a minute. I'm not putting up with all this sexism. Hang on. I'll be out in a minute.'

I tapped my foot impatiently. It seemed ages before the door opened and Dad appeared swathed in a huge bath towel. I followed him to his room. 'What does your mum think?' he demanded, rubbing his hair.

'Oh, she thinks he's lovely. He's wowed her with his Parisian charm and his husky voice. *And* he's brought her this huge box of French chocolates.'

'Obviously a young man of great discernment. I shall have to watch my step. Can't have a young Gallic charmer sweeping my wife off her feet. Has he brought perfume and flowers as well?'

'No—but there is some red wine.'

'Can this boy do no wrong? I must meet him straightaway and shake him by the hand.'

'Dad! Be serious! I want you to get rid of him! What good's a boy going to be with two babies? He'll be more trouble than he's worth!'

'*Pourquoi?*'

'Dad!' I stamped my foot, I was so exasperated.

'Dear me, Kate,' said Dad mildly.

'And you're the one who always complains when people assume that it's your mum who's the hairdresser and your dad who's the vicar. Why on earth shouldn't a boy be any good with babies?'

I glowered at him. Dad's brilliant with them himself, of course. One look at him and they go ga-ga. I'd forgotten that.

'Well, there aren't many men like you,' I muttered. 'Dominique's hardly likely to be one of them.'

'Dominique? Is that his name?'

'Yes—though he says to call him Nic. That's how Mum made the mistake. I mean, it could be a girl's name, couldn't it? It can be either in France. Mum just assumed all along that he was a girl. When she got the form out again to look, he'd quite clearly ringed the M for male.'

'I see. You'd think there'd be something else to give it away—but I can't remember anything myself.'

'No—it's all in sort of note form. You know—"likes working with children, has taken a preliminary first aid course, accomplished cellist"—that sort of thing. And the referees have just signed that they agree with it all.'

'Aha! And presumably he hasn't got a sore throat—that's his normal voice.'

'That's right.'

'Well, that's sorted then. Pass me the talc, please, Kate.' I watched the cloud of powder settle on the carpet and groaned.

'You see,' I said. I wasn't prepared to give in that easily. 'Men! You've just got no idea about mess!'

'Kate, since when have you hoovered my bedroom?' Dad fixed me with a steely eye.

'Um . . . well . . .'

'Never! All right? So don't come whingeing to me because this Dominique is a boy. I'm sure he'll be fine. The last I heard, you were all steamed up at the thought of some exotic European seducing Ben! Let's give him a chance, shall we? You never know—God might have a very good reason for all of this. His methods are often mysterious.'

'Yes, well that figures, doesn't it?' I

snarled. 'God's yet another man!'

'Not necessarily!' Dad called after me, as I stamped down the stairs. But I was too annoyed to answer back.

*   *   *

I half-thought all that racing up to London and the shock about Nic would start off Mum's labour—but no such luck. It's got to the stage now that we'll all be heartily glad when the twins arrive, even if they are the babies from hell. Nothing could be worse than BTM the way she is. Talk about a short fuse! Poor Nic must be ruing the day he applied for this job. At first I could barely manage to be civil to him but with BTM being as foul as she knows how, I simply had to unbend a bit.

And of course, Dad was right as usual. Nic's so nice it almost makes you sick—and his English is really quite good, so it's not that difficult to talk to him. And he's so tidy! At first, I thought he was just trying to make a good impression but after three weeks there are still no nail-clippings left on the side of the bath or any extra coffee cups growing mould around the place. The embarrassing fact is that he's about a hundred times tidier than any of us. He'd get on well with Carly. No—sorry I said that. He may be always neat and clean but he doesn't have that awful air of 'don't-come-near-you-might-contaminate-me'. Can't think how Carly can bear to let Chas touch her actually. I'd have thought she might be worried he'd get pig-poo in her hair.

Talking of poo, Nic has a great sense of humour. Something awful happened to him today. Well, I'd have died if it had happened to me. It was an awful day for me too, which is why I'm hammering away at this keyboard, but I'll come to that later.

We were invited to Sunday lunch with the Petersons and BTM agreed at the speed of light, despite the groans from Ben and me. Much as we love Chas, an afternoon playing dinner-parties with his family is a major strain. The meal goes on for ever and you have to make endless polite conversation. Apart from that, relations between me and Chas have been non-existent since our awful fight. I wasn't at all sure that I wanted to spend a whole afternoon in his company—and worse, what if Carly was there too?

But BTM was determined and Dad was keen too. The meals are getting pretty erratic in our house at the moment. BTM can barely reach the hot-plates now and certainly can't bend to put anything in the oven, so we're trying to share out the meals between us. Dad's a great cook but gets in late and Ben and I aren't exactly adventurous. Nic is used to cooking with gas and after three attempts at omelettes on our ancient electric hob and three suppers à la charcoal, he's not keen to try again.

'*C'est impossible!*' he says and I'm inclined to agree. I hate omelettes anyway.

So the chance of a roast dinner chez Mrs Charming Peterson was too tempting to resist. By the time we got there after church, you could almost see the drool hanging out of Dad's mouth.

I half expected Mrs Peterson to be a fluent French speaker and to whisk Nic off for *un aperitif dans le jardin.* But no—*la belle France* may be one of her favourite countries but her French is *très mal.* *Très* very *mal*, actually. She would keep trying it out. Chas kept wincing (bet he was glad Carly *hadn't* been invited) and Nic kept smiling an endearing, slightly puzzled smile.

It was after the main course that Nic dropped his clanger. Mrs Charming was just bringing in the pudding, a gloriously sticky steamed treacle sponge.

'Especially *pour tu*,' she trilled at poor Nic. 'A pudding *très Anglais!*'

He smiled but looked uncomfortable. 'Excuse me,' he said, 'but where is the poo?'

Mrs Peterson froze. I'm surprised she didn't drop the pudding.

'I'm sorry?' she said, her smile a little forced.

Why one of us didn't work out what

he meant and come to the rescue, I will never know. I suppose we were all as bemused as Mrs Charming Peterson.

'The poo,' repeated Nic, clearly sensing that something was wrong. 'I'm sorry—is that not right? I would like to go to the poo.'

I think everyone burst out laughing at once, even Gran, who always manages to stay awake to eat. Everyone except me. And poor Nic, of course. He did try. And he thought it was very funny later. But right that moment, he had such a look of the wounded spaniel, that the laughter died in my throat.

'Come on,' I said, leaping up. 'I'll show you. They're just idiots. It was obvious you meant the loo.'

*   *   *

It was a beautiful late September afternoon. BTM can usually be persuaded to go out to see Mr Peterson's pigs but she can barely walk a hundred paces at the moment without needing resuscitation. Gran was snoring almost before the coffee had been cleared away and Chas and Ben wanted to go to the outhouse to play darts. Chas and I had been skirting round each other like boxers waiting for the first punch. So it was Dad and Mr Peterson and Nic and me who set off up the hill in our wellies.

It was lovely to have a chance to get to know Nic a bit better. The few weeks since he arrived have been very busy. He's had to learn to find his way around and about all the peculiarities of our domestic appliances. He's started an English class at the college and seems to spend every spare moment practising the cello. Meanwhile, I've had to get used to my new teachers, who all seem to have started the term by giving us hours of homework. So we haven't had much time to talk. And anyway, he seems quite shy.

We got on fine. We laughed about the poo-loo thing and that really broke the ice. Nic was soon telling me all about himself. He's got a place at university to read music in a year's time but he'd really like to join an orchestra that tours internationally, which is why he's so keen to improve his English.

'But what about the babies?' I said. 'Won't you find them a bit of a pain?' He sounded such a sensitive soul, I couldn't imagine him coping with two screaming brats.

He smiled comfortably. 'Babies,' he said. 'They love me. And I love them.'

He's probably right. He can probably tickle two at once with one hand.

*   *   *

I was surprised to find Chas lurking in the kitchen when we got back from our walk.

'Where's Ben?' I said.

'Playing on the computer. Would you like a drink?' He sounded painfully polite.

'Mmm. Yes please. Shall I ask the others?'

They had all disappeared into the sitting room. I was quickly back with their orders.

'So,' said Chas, looking sideways at

me, as he spooned tea into the pot. 'The au pair isn't so bad after all. He certainly seems to be getting on very well with you.'

I laughed. The fresh air had relaxed me. 'Yes, all right, I take it all back—having an au pair was a good idea. You can say "I told you so" if you want.'

'I told you so.'

We grinned at each other.

'But,' said Chas, 'what if he had been a girl?'

'So? What if he had?'

'Wouldn't that have been a bit different? I thought you were dead worried about having an exotic European swanning around your house?'

'Oh, I was just panicking. I'm sure it'd have been fine.'

'Yeah?'

I began to smell a rat. 'Look, Chas, is there something you're trying to get at? Because if there is, just say it, will you? All right?'

'Oh, it's nothing.'

'No, it isn't. You're definitely trying to have a go at me—but I can't imagine what it's about.'

'No—really,' said Chas breezily. 'It's nothing. I just thought, you know, hunky, charming French bloke—a bit different from what you were expecting. Almost bound to win you over, I should say.'

I stared at Chas furiously. If he'd given me my tea, I'd have thrown it at him. The red mist descended with a vengeance; I could feel the colour racing to my cheeks.

'I can't believe you just said that, Chas Peterson,' I said, my voice trembling. 'Of all the snide . . . oh, it's not even worth bothering to say anything.'

I turned on my heel but Chas grabbed my arm.

'Hey, Kate, I was only teasing—I just thought . . . well, he does seem the sort of bloke . . .'

'Chas, he's *eighteen*! I'm not stupid enough to think he'd even look at me, let alone . . . I'd never even given *that* a thought! You're obsessed with sex! Anyway, you weren't teasing, you were having a go at me. And I don't know why! Ever since that stupid Carly arrived, you've been out to get me. And I thought you were my best friend!'

'Don't drag Carly into this! It's nothing to do with her. It's ever since your mum got pregnant. You haven't been the same person at all. You're always whingeing and you've got no sense of humour whatsoever. If you want my opinion, you need to see a shrink!'

'Well, I *don't* want your opinion, so why don't you just shut up!'

We stood glaring at each other, the kitchen table separating us or I think I'd have throttled him with a damp tea-towel.

At this interesting point, in walked Ben, with Nic close behind him.

Ben raised his eyebrows. 'Uh-oh,' he said grinning. 'What's this? A little tiff?'

That did it. A brother is born for adversity? Forget it! I grabbed the sugar pot (it was silver, fortunately), flung it at Ben and swore at him. Mum has yet another helpful verse she's drummed into us for occasions like these. 'A gentle answer turns away

wrath but a harsh word stirs up anger.'
Oh well, blown it again. Someone,
somewhere, needs to pray harder for
me.

11

My Mum Goes Walkabout

Have you ever had to clean up sugar?
Great, isn't it? No matter how much
you sweep, it's still going crunch and
sticking to your feet three hours later.
Mrs Peterson gave me a bucket of
scalding water when I'd finished with
the broom but I reckon all that did was
make syrup on her floor.

Anyway, Mrs Charming's sticky floor
is the least of our worries. That was
yesterday, and it's certainly true that
each day has enough worries of its own.
I'm sitting here trying to take my mind
off the fact that Mum has disappeared.
Disappeared! Mum! Seems a bit
incredible the size she is and the speed
she can move at the moment—she

doesn't even fit in the car any more—but disappeared she has. We've searched and we've prayed and we've rung everyone we can think of. I can't stand it any longer, so here I am, tapping away, waiting for my prayers to be answered. Perhaps if I could manage to pray *before* there's a crisis my life wouldn't be continually out of control.

Mum is out of control. Definitely. When I got home from school today, she was haranguing someone down the telephone.

'What I am saying is that the tumble-dryer, which used to make a high-pitched whining noise, has now stopped doing it. And since your man was supposed to come to fix it this morning, I'd like you to cancel the call-out.'

I could see from the way she was clutching the receiver that she was imagining it was someone's neck, so I quietly put the kettle on and lurked out of missile range.

'I don't care if he's on his way—he should have been and gone by now, and since he hasn't, I would like you to cancel the call. Is that clear? Right. Thank you.'

She put down the phone. 'Honestly,' she spat. 'Some people.'

The kettle was almost boiling now so I wasn't quite sure but . . .

'Mum,' I said. 'I thought you told that woman the tumble-dryer had *stopped* making a high-pitched whining noise?'

'It has. That's what's so irritating. It's been doing it for weeks and then, suddenly, I put it on this afternoon and it was as silent as the grave.'

The kettle clicked itself off. 'I don't think . . .' I began tentatively.

BTM snatched open the door of our tiny utility room. There was an unmistakable whine. Anyone would have thought she was tumble-drying Frisk.

'I don't believe it,' said BTM. 'I simply don't believe it. I've just cancelled the call out because I don't want a forty-pound bill for nothing and now listen to it! Incredible!'

'Um—what are you going to do?' I

150

asked nervously.

'Do? I'm going to ring that silly woman back, of course, and tell her to send a man out after all! What else is there to do?'

I picked up my mug of coffee and escaped. I did not want to be a witness to this. Most normal human beings wouldn't have the face to demand that their tumble-dryer should still be mended today but I knew Mum had— and just being in the same room would make me want to curl up and die. Perhaps that's why BTM's so keen on Bible verses about taming the tongue and gentle answers turning away wrath—she knows she's a complete failure at both!

Anyway, I retreated to the lounge to watch TV for a bit before starting my homework. From upstairs I could hear Nic practising his cello—very soothing. I almost forgot the caged tiger rampaging round the kitchen—well, until I heard the sound of breaking glass, that is.

Nic pounded down the stairs, I burst out of the lounge, we crashed in the hall and then reeled into the kitchen. Ben was standing in the garden, ashen-faced, and BTM, hands on what had once been her hips, was yelling at him as if he was stone-deaf and at least half. a mile away. Between them swung the kitchen door, a jagged hole where its window had been only moments before.

Nic and I were speechless. BTM wasn't though.

'Now look what you've made me do!' she yelled. 'As if leaving all your smelly, filthy, disgusting football kit on the table weren't enough, now you've gone and made me smash a window!'

With that, she burst into tears, pushed Nic and me aside and stormed out of the room.

Then Ben began to cry. Stunned, I stepped over the heap of broken glass and dragged him in.

'All I did was put my dirty football kit on the table and she went ballistic,' he sobbed. 'She pushed me back into the garden, yelling something about "how dare I when she hasn't even got a working tumble-dryer", then she slammed the door and the glass fell out!'

I hugged him. 'I think she's had a bad day,' I said. 'It's not you. It's the babies. If she doesn't have them soon, she'll completely lose her marbles.'

'I thought she was going to kill me!'

Between us, Nic and I got Ben to calm down. He usually takes things in his stride but this time he was seriously upset. You could tell because he ate three of the chocolate biscuits which Nic found, despite his anti-spot campaign. Then we started to clear up the mess.

Just then the doorbell rang. The man for the tumble-dryer—well, of course.

'D'you still want me?' he demanded grumpily. 'I was only a few miles away when I got a call to say you didn't—and the next minute, I got another to say you did! What's going on?'

'I'm not sure,' I said. 'I'll check with Mum.'

It was then that we realized that she'd gone.

*   *   *

I'm too young for this. I told the repair man to do what he had to do—seeing as he'd arrived, it was going to cost us forty quid anyway—then I rang Dad, and on his advice, started to ring round glaziers to get some estimates for the window

'Hang on in there, Kate,' Dad told me. 'I'll get home as soon as I can. Send Ben and Nic out to look for her. She can't have gone far.'

Oh no? That was two and a half hours ago and we still haven't found her. Suzie's joined us, and so have several neighbours and Mum's boss, the vicar. Dad insisted that we had a break for something to eat so Nic and I went to get fish and chips but it was a waste of money; none of us really felt like eating. Dad rang the hospital fairly early on, in case she'd been found and carted off there, so our nerves are trigger-happy, hoping for a phone-call. It's at times like these that I really miss Chas. I'd love to ring him and pour it all out—no, that's silly—if things were like they used to be, he'd be here helping to look and I wouldn't be stuck here, bashing away at this stupid keyboard. It's driving me nuts but I can't think of anything else to do. Dad's phoning the police and everyone else is back out looking but I'm scared that if I stop typing I'll run mad and start foaming at the mouth or something. One completely batty person per family is enough, I think.

Hang on! Wait a minute! Maybe that's it! Batty! Bats! Belfry! Mum loves the belfry. One of her ex-crazes is bell-ringing. She loves the atmosphere up there—says it's eerie but peaceful. But could she get up there? In her condition? The size she is? Surely not? I'd better tell Dad though—just in case . . .

*   *   *

That's where she was of course. Fast asleep. We all charged down to the church, the vicar and Dad sprinting at least as fast as Olympic medallists. By the time I'd panted to a halt, they were already staging the rescue. The spiral stairs are steep and narrow so getting up there must have taken Mum a superhuman effort. Ben said anything was possible—she threw him out of the back door like Superwoman—but we almost needed Superman to drag her back down.

'I can't see my feet,' she kept complaining as Dad and the vicar (whose name, by the way, is Simon), slowly manoeuvred her down, one in front and one behind.

Dear me, she did look a state. All tear-stained and dusty and blotchy-faced.

'Oh Ben, I am sorry,' she said, nearly suffocating him in a bear hug and promptly bursting into tears again.

'All right, that's enough,' said Dad gruffly—he tends to get a bit shirty when he's been upset. 'I want to get you down to the hospital to be checked over.'

'Oh no,' moaned Mum. 'I'll be fine now. I just needed to be on my own for a bit.'

'Fine?' Dad exploded. 'Fine? You're completely unhinged, woman! What did you think you were doing, going and hiding in the belfry? If you want to be on your own, the loo will do! Now be quiet and do as you're told.'

He got his way. I think Mum was too exhausted and embarrassed to argue, especially when she saw that the police dog-handlers had arrived at our house. So now I'm waiting to see what happens next. Dad rang a couple of hours ago to say the midwives wanted to keep an eye on her. Perhaps I should pace the floor a bit, like they do in those old movies.

*   *   *

At last! They've arrived. The twins are finally here. They're huge—6lbs 12oz and 7lbs 2oz. Can you believe it? It's not surprising poor old Mum has been so irritable. Fancy dragging that lot round all the time! Dad says all that barmy behaviour was because of the labour starting off. I suppose taking yourself off to the belfry isn't that much more peculiar than making a nest in Ben's sock drawer. Anyway, within half an hour of getting to the hospital, Mum's waters broke and then things really got going. Only a couple of hours later and they were born—no complications, just lots of sweat.

'Did she scream much?' I demanded.

'No,' said Dad, 'but you should see the bruises on my wrists.'

Anyway, I'm going to hit the sack now. Thank God they're safely here—I mean that—and that BTM hasn't been carted off to the funny farm. I need to make the most of the peace and quiet—bet it's the last I get for a while.

The babies haven't got names yet—Mum and Dad can't decide. Dad asked me if I'd got any ideas. I can bore myself off to sleep thinking of some. It'd be easy if they were both boys. Jacob and Esau, or how about Ant and Dec?! But they're not. And I'm not sure what I think about this bit yet. I hadn't really expected this to happen. They're girls. Both of them. Oh well, at least they won't pee on the bathroom floor—or not once they're potty-trained anyway.

12

My Mum and the Gruesome Twosome

Yikes! Why did I ever think things would be better when the twins were born? BTM is—she's obviously never heard of the baby blues—but I think I'm having her share.

'Well, they're better out than in,' she says with monotonous regularity. Maybe they are—for her! But for the rest of us! Aargh! Even Nic, who 'loves' babies, is a bit frazzled. Anyway, he's getting a lot of cello practice done—it's about the only thing that shuts them up. That and feeding.

BTM's boobs have exploded. I reckon she could feed an army with the amount of milk she's producing. So why are my darling little sisters never satisfied? I reckon it's jealousy. You're convinced one of them must be so full she'll burst, but her roving eye only has to catch sight of her twin tucking in and all hell lets loose. Mum tries to feed them together whenever possible but they lie there, glaring balefully at each other, willing the other to stop first—and, of course, neither of them will. They're determined little so-and-sos, I'll say that for them.

I lost on the breastfeeding front, of course. And I can just about see the advantages now. It's certainly far more convenient to just pull up your T-shirt and get on with it, than have to make up all those bottles—especially in the middle of the night. And Mum's so casual about it, you stop noticing. At least it's one thing I can't do for them. I can change nappies—I could change nappies for England. No one ever told me about baby poo. I couldn't believe it at first—it's bright yellow and goes *everywhere*. Nic, Ben and I are getting pretty competitive about how we put nappies on. You lose points if one of them leaks—so I'm not at all keen on BTM's latest bright idea. She wants to change to washable nappies. Washable! Aargh! As if things weren't bad enough!

'Kate, don't you have any concern for the environment?' she says. 'Don't you know that disposable nappies take up massive amounts of landfill and take up to a hundred years to rot?'

'Can't you burn them?'

'And add to the greenhouse effect? Nice one, Kate!'

'But what about all the hot water and detergent it takes to wash nappies? That must be bad for the environment too!'

'Not as bad as the alternative. And don't forget the expense of disposables. Come on, Kate. It's not like in the old days when you'd have had to wash them by hand. It really isn't such a big deal. God has given us this beautiful world; it's up to us to look after it.'

Huh! Looks like we're doomed then. I wonder if she'd be quite so keen if she didn't have a small army of mugs to help her! There's one good thing though—it proves she's back to normal. I never thought I'd say this but I can honestly say that I'm glad the real BTM is back.

So what should we call her now?

BTM or BBM? Her tummy's deflated a bit but I doubt if it'll ever be the same again. You should see those stretch marks! Reminds me of an elephant's bottom. Yikes—another of the joys of childbirth to look forward to. I shall definitely become a nun.

*   *   *

How much worse can it get? Will those babies never stop crying? I think even BTM, who has been running on adrenalin for three weeks, is beginning to feel the strain. My theory is that it's the younger one that's got the problem and she sets the other one off. If big sister gets a cuddle, then she wants one too. And they both always want Mum. They'll make do with Nic or Ben or Dad or me—until they see that someone else has got a better deal. There're loads of babies at church who sit quietly in their car-seats and gurgle—these two, not a chance!

We've tried everything we can think of. Dummies (they spit them out), baby colic drops (they're sick), baby massage (they scream as soon as you start undoing their babygros), leaving them in the garden (the neighbours complain), taking them for long drives (they scream even louder). I considered suggesting that we tried giving them a bottle but it's more than my life's worth. Anyway, they're obviously not hungry—they're piling on weight like Sumo wrestlers. BTM thinks they're bored, so Nic's been making mobiles out of milk bottle tops but it's all hopeless. Even his cello is beginning to lose its magical effect. We've all got bags under our eyes and might as well be a family of crocodiles, we snap so much.

*   *   *

At last! They've got names! Apart from the monsters, the gruesome twosome, the babies from hell etc. etc. Dad wanted names from the Bible and Mum didn't—so they've chosen one each. Same happened with us—that's why I'm Kate and Ben is Benjamin. Anyway, the new two are Hayley and

Rebekah.

'We wanted names that are completely different,' explained Mum, 'and we don't mind nicknames as long as they're not silly—so Rebekah can be Becky, if you like.'

At that moment, Rebekah, who had just pulled away from Mum's breast, gave a huge hiccup and powered a great stream of milk in an arc across the wall.

'Yikes!' I said. 'Is that normal?'

'Ha!' chortled Ben. 'You should call her Comet. Like Halley's Comet!'

If Mum hadn't got her arms full of baby, I think she'd have hit him—she contented herself with sending him for a cloth to clean up the mess. But we won't forget. Comet by nature, so she'll be Comet by name. Hayley and Comet! Nice one, Ben! Got to get our revenge somehow.

*   *   *

Well, I didn't get *any* sleep last night. Hayley and Comet belly-ached the whole time. Actually, it was mostly

Comet. Nic and Ben seemed to manage to snore through it but me, I'm too sensitive! Every so often there'd be a lull and I'd begin to drowse off, only to be jerked awake by another furious scream. I kept popping out to see if there was anything I could do but Mum and Dad insisted that I needed my sleep! Joke! Couldn't they tell that the way I kept reappearing proved I wasn't getting any? I got hopeful when Dad took the twins out for a drive. He was gone for a whole hour and I think Mum crashed out but I didn't. I just lay there, stiff as a board, worrying about how we're going to cope. I can't believe this is normal. Anyway, in the end Dad was forced back to the house because he couldn't bear it any longer—they were still screaming. How on earth do they manage to keep it up?

At around four o'clock, Hayley finally gave up. I reckon she'd just been upset by her sister. But Comet went on and on. At about quarter past five, I was appalled to hear Mum join in. I crept along to her bedroom to find Comet lying screaming on the double bed and Mum and Dad locked in each others' arms.

I think even Dad was crying.

'Go and ring the doctor, Kate,' he said. 'I'm convinced this is something serious.'

The doctor came. Poor man—it was absolutely pouring with rain. He got drenched just staggering in from the car. Mum answered the door.

'Is this your first baby?' he enquired sympathetically.

'No!' she snorted. It's my fourth!'

'Ah. Well, let's take a look, shall we?'

Well, he looked—but he didn't find anything.

'She seems perfectly healthy,' he said at last. 'Could she be hungry?'

If Dad hadn't been there to hold her back, I think Mum would have thumped the doctor.

'I've been feeding her nearly all *night*,' she spat. 'And that's just the trouble! Now she won't feed! Look!'

Mum snatched up Comet and pulled her in close. To my absolute amazement, she arched her back, pulled away and *screamed*!

'Hmm. I see what you mean,' said the doctor. 'Have you tried a bo . . .?'

'Bath?' I interrupted. Mentioning bottle-feeding was more than his life was worth—but how could he know that no bottle is ever to touch the precious darlings' lips? 'Have we tried a bath?' I continued. 'Yes, they tried that about two hours ago.' I could just see it—headline news: VICIOUS VICAR DUFFS UP DOCTOR. In the mood she was in, after a sleepless night, anything was possible.

'No, I meant a . . .' Fortunately, the doctor wasn't stupid. He could see Dad and me glaring at him. 'Ahem,' he said. 'I meant a hot-water bottle. On her tummy. Wrapped up, of course. Very soothing.'

'We've tried that,' said Dad wearily. 'She hated it.'

The doctor clearly didn't want to leave but it was terribly obvious that there was nothing he could do.

'I'm sure she'll settle down soon,' he said. 'If she's no better in the morning . . . (what was he *talking* about? This *was* the morning) . . . then ring the

167

surgery.'

We said goodbye politely. I showed him out. It was still pouring with rain. Upstairs, Comet was still screaming. A baby carrier was hanging on the pegs with our coats. I made a decision. I grabbed it and ran upstairs.

'I'm taking her out,' I announced.

'Give me a minute while I get dressed.'

'But you'll get soaked,' protested Mum. 'And so will Rebekah.'

'I don't care. I'll take an umbrella.'

I think Mum and Dad were past caring too. Neither of them said anything more and when I returned in my jeans and a sweatshirt, they helped me strap Comet to my chest in the carrier. I zipped up my cagoule round her so that only the top of her head showed. She was still screaming, but her cries were muffled because her mouth was squashed up against my chest. That'll teach you, I thought grimly.

'Right,' I said. 'You get some sleep. I'm off.'

They didn't argue so I tramped down the stairs, found my wellies and the

168

biggest brolly we have and opened the front door.

The sheer wetness took my breath away. If I hadn't had the umbrella to protect me, I seriously wonder if I'd have had enough air to breath. Ever walked under a waterfall? It was like that. I couldn't hear Comet any more because of the pounding on my umbrella. I hoped it was strong enough to withstand the rain.

Anyway, Comet seemed to like it. As I struggled along the road, I could feel her beginning to relax. I peered down at her. She was straining to get her face free and as I watched, she peered up at me, her brow puckered with the effort. I was expecting her to look angry but her deep blue eyes looked more bewildered than anything else. I plodded on, watching her, and as I walked her eyelids gradually began to close. I could feel her warm little body nestling into me and a very strange thing began to happen. For the first time, I started to feel protective towards her. I had taken her out because we were desperate—because

169

we needed some sleep. Now, and I'd never really thought of it before, I wanted to know *why* she kept crying. What was upsetting her so much? What a life! Three weeks on this earth and she'd done nothing but scream and feed. I was actually beginning to feel sorry for her.

Just then, I heard my name called and started. Comet's eyelids jerked open and she grimaced at me.

'Kate! Is that you under there? You're out early, aren't you?'

It was Suzie, being hauled along by a huge dog.

'So are you. I didn't know you had a dog! Isn't it a bit wet for him to be out?' Seven children and a dog! How did they cope?

Suzie grinned—or I think she did. I couldn't see much of her for the hood of her jacket. 'He's not mine. He belongs to my grandad—but he's ill at the moment and Monty doesn't care about the weather. Who've you got there?'

'Comet—I mean, Rebekah.'

'Oh, call her Comet. Ben told me all

170

about that. She's the screamer, isn't she?'

'Well, Hayley's almost as bad—but Comet's been at it *all night*!'

'You should take her to a cranial osteopath if she's that bad. Mum did with Freddie. He was terrible—and he was loads better, straightaway.'

'What on earth is a—what did you say again?'

'A cranial osteopath. They do this kind of head massage. I think it sort of rearranges their heads—you know, in case they got squashed when they were born.'

'I bet Hayley and Comet did! They were enormous—for twins.'

'Tell your mum to give it a go, then. You never know, it might work miracles.'

'I think Mum's *praying* for a miracle, actually.'

'I'm sure God wouldn't mind a little help,' said Suzie brightly. 'Anyway, I'd better go. This old pooch is soaked and I'll have to dry him.'

Suddenly, I felt unaccountably cheerful. I think I approve of Ben's taste in girls; it's certainly working out a lot better than mine in boys. I've barely seen Chas since the twins were born. That awful scene we had in his kitchen is still on my mind—but I've been too busy and tired to do anything about it. I've thought of trying to catch him at school but he's always got Carly with him and I just haven't had the guts. Anyway, I strode along the road, splashing in the puddles, a real spring in my step. Comet seemed to have dozed off properly but I didn't want to stop in case she woke up again. I could walk for miles if I had to—well, that's what I thought until my brolly blew inside out.

The rain had slackened when it happened and I hadn't been expecting the sudden gust that did it. Have you ever tried getting an umbrella the right way out with a sleeping baby strapped to you? Easier said than done. Comet was beginning to squawk again and I was getting truly desperate when a car pulled up beside me. That was all I needed—to be mugged as well. I started to walk briskly away when, for the second time that morning, I heard my name called.

This time it was Simon, the vicar, Mum's boss.

'Can I help?' he asked. 'I'm just off shopping but you look like you could do with a hand.'

'Shopping? At this time in the morning?'

He shrugged. 'It's a busy life. But it's not often I meet someone out with a baby this early. Which one is it?'

I told him. Then I told him about our awful night. By this stage I was sitting in the passenger seat next to him. Comet began to whimper again. So I joined in.

'Shall I take you home?' said Simon.

'No,' I sobbed. 'Mum and Dad need to sleep. It's because I've stopped moving. But I can't keep walking without my umbrella. And anyway, Comet isn't allowed in a car without her proper car-seat.'

Simon looked thoughtful for a moment or two and then felt in his pocket. He handed me a bunch of keys. 'Go to the church,' he said. 'There's heaps of space to walk up and down in there. I'll see how you're getting on when I get back.'

I looked at him, unsure.

'Go on, Kate. You're a hero. I hope my little girls turn out like you.'

I think that's the nicest thing anyone's ever said to me. It kept my spirits up all the way to the church, even though Comet was yelling because rain was trickling down her face. Once I'd got in, I wiped her with a soggy tissue and I think she almost smiled. Then I did what Simon had suggested. I walked up and down. It was very boring so I tried singing. After all, Comet likes music. It sounded brilliant—I'm not a bad singer and my voice sounded huge in all that empty space. I sang all my favourites—everything I know off by heart—and then I picked up a hymn book and started on them. Comet drowsed off very quickly but I was having such a lovely time that I went on and on till I was hoarse. There was something incredibly soothing about stomping around, singing my heart out, a cosy, velvet-headed bundle keeping me warm, while the rain pounded on the ancient roof. In the end, I sat down in a pew, ever so carefully in case Comet decided to wake up. She didn't—and that was where Simon found me, my head slumped against hers, a hymn book open on my lap.

He shook me gently. 'Wake up, Kate. I'm taking you back to the vicarage for some breakfast. I've stuck a note through your door to say where you are. All the curtains are still drawn.'

He grabbed the hymn book just before I stood up and let it crash to the floor.

'Hey!' he said. 'Look where it was open. This is what you need, isn't it, Kate?'

I glanced at where his finger was pointing—some lines from an old hymn.

Mornings of joy give for evenings of tearfulness,
Trust for our trembling and hope for our fear.

I smiled and looked down at Comet, nestling pink-cheeked against me. I could feel the gentle rise and fall as she breathed peacefully. My baby sister. We had been through something special together.

'This is a morning of joy,' I said.

13

My Mum Goes Shopping

Well, the bad news is that one lovey-dovey morning with a baby doesn't solve everything. Life goes on. By the time we got home, Comet was wet and stinky and so was my sweatshirt. But at least she fed, and then slept for another couple of hours. Dad staggered off to work, Ben breezed off to school, Nic tackled a huge pile of ironing (what a star!) and Mum and I sloped back to bed for a while.

The good news is that Mum took the babies to the cranial osteopath—and it worked! As soon as I told her about it she was on the phone and got an appointment for that afternoon. I'm not saying there was a complete transformation—I reckon Comet will be touchy for the rest of her life—but at least she's bearable now. And there's a very noticeable knock-on effect on Hayley too. You think 'nasty but normal' rather than 'babies from hell' now. Miracle rating? Not at all bad. BTM's convinced it's an answer to prayer, Suzie is crowing because she thought of it, but secretly, I think it was all that singing I did in the church. My bet is that Comet will turn out to be a musical genius.

Anyway, all that was weeks ago. Nic is a godsend and Suzie is lovely (she doesn't natter on so much now she's got used to us) so the only fly in the ointment is that I really miss Chas. And let's face it, I'm still jealous. How can he prefer hanging around with Cute Carly instead of me? I know what I ought to do. I ought to just march up to him and apologize for being so rude and see what happens—but whenever I think of it, he's with Carly and I start thinking he ought to apologize first. After all, it was him winding me up

177

about Nic that started it. 'A friend loves at all times.' Huh! I wish Dad had never told me that!

*   *   *

Aargh! Aargh! Aargh! I want to curl up and die! I thought I'd got past this! I thought I'd grown out of being so embarrassed that I want to hide my head in a bucket and scream! Aargh!

I went shopping with BTM. Mistake. She does the ordinary shopping with Nic but this was special. She wanted to buy some clothes—she's lost so much weight with feeding the babies. Anyway, she needed to be baby-free to try things on, but she had to take them with her in case they needed her. Nic wanted to go shopping too, so we packed them into the baby-carriers and set off. BTM was skipping about like a three-year-old. The thought of an hour without any babies had clearly gone to her head. Not to mention the thought of new clothes. I dreaded to think what she might buy but I've given up commenting on her appalling taste.

We agreed to split and meet by the fountain in an hour. The babies had just been fed so we reckoned we'd be safe, especially as BTM has started them on solids. (Question: why do they call it 'starting on solids', when it's actually starting on mush? To my mind, something solid is steak and chips, not a teaspoonful of mashed banana!) Nic wandered off to scour the music stores, BTM bolted into the nearest boutique with a SALE sign and I stayed where I was. I'm broke and Comet seemed very happy to watch the fountain.

I was chatting away to her as you do with babies and making great fountain gestures with my arms (she liked that) when I suddenly had the feeling that I was being watched. I glanced round and, sure enough, there was Cute Carly, perched daintily on the opposite wall, having a snide grin to herself. Well, I'm above that sort of thing. I smiled and waved—and then didn't know what to do next. My happy stream of nonsense came to an abrupt halt, as did the arm waving. Should I go over and speak to her, or quietly disappear into the crowd? I didn't fancy the latter. Somehow, it would make me feel she'd won—though won what, heaven only knows. A fountain-watching contest? Comet was getting restless—she didn't like the break in her entertainment—so that settled it. Casually, I started walking over—just as Chas hurried out of McDonald's.

He stopped when he saw me, the packet of 'fries' he was offering to Carly frozen in his hand.

'Hi Kate,' he said awkwardly. He could hardly ignore me.

'Hi.'

Silence.

'Who's that you've got there then?'

'Comet—I mean, Rebekah.' I wanted to cry. We'd been so close and he didn't even know about Comet.

'Oh, Ben told me about her. The puke on the wall and all that. She's the difficult one, isn't she?'

I fired up. I think it was the dreaded jealousy again. Of course, he's still friends with Ben—even though he's hardly ever round at our house any more. Well, who would want to be? It isn't just me—it's even more chaotic than ever.

'Hayley's not exactly a bundle of laughs either, you know!' I snapped. 'And you shouldn't label people—especially not twins. It's bad enough being a twin as it is.'

Oh, why don't I just go and tear out my tongue and fry it? There I was, moaning again. Always so negative—and he was only trying to be friendly.

Well, I got my just desserts. I was struggling to think of some light-hearted, jolly little witticism to make up for being so snotty, when Comet, who had been getting distinctly restless, made the most disgustingly loud squelch. I looked down in horror. Whoever put on her nappy that morning scored negative points—either that or the famous solids had disagreed with her. Solid was the last word I would have used. I had my jacket on but it was a mild day so it wasn't fastened. How I wished it was—then at least Cute Carly wouldn't have had a full-view of the brownish-yellow slime which Comet jet-propelled down the legs of her babygro. It was even leaking through—and worse, I could see that she was summoning up all her forces to produce more!

Chas (the friend I love at all times, remember?) couldn't stop laughing. 'I can see why you call her Comet!' he choked. 'Oh sorry, Kate, I know I shouldn't but . . .'

'Oh shut up!' I said. 'No, Comet—not more!' I was clutching my jacket round her. Bad mistake—it was leaking out of her babygro toes. It was then that I realized Nic had gone off with the changing bag.

'Oh sh . . .!'

'You can say that again!' chortled Chas. Really! You can go off some people rapidly. Nonetheless, a small corner of my horrified brain was delighted to see that Cute Carly was regarding him disdainfully.

'Oh, grow up, Chas!' she hissed. 'Let's go!'

Chas looked at her in surprise. 'Don't be silly,' he said. 'We can't go and leave Kate in this mess.'

'Well, you sort it out then,' she

sneered. 'I'll meet you at Miss Selfridge in half an hour.'

Miss Selfridge! Chas! What had he turned into? Some sort of posh girl's footman? Did he hold the bags while she tried things on? I stared at him in astonishment.

'She wants me to help her choose something,' he said and blushed. 'Anyway, can I help? That can't be worse than pig poo.'

Our eyes met. I laughed. Oh Chas! I thought. I have missed you.

'I don't know,' I said. 'I can't think what to do. Nic's got the changing bag—and I'm not due to meet him for another three-quarters of an hour. And I've got about 15p in my purse—not even enough for one nappy.'

'Well, I've got a bit of cash. I'm sure they'd let you have a nappy and stuff at one of those baby shops—and I could buy a cheap babygro.'

'I bet we could get one from a charity shop.'

'Are you sure? Would you mind that?' Chas looked anxious.

'Don't be silly. I get some of my best

stuff from charity shops. And it's good recycling too.' It was on the tip of my tongue to say something cutting about Carly—I mean, can you imagine her wearing anything second-hand?—but I managed to stop myself just in time. I'm learning.

I zipped up my jacket—hot and smelly but better than giving the public the full benefit—and we set off. We had a great time. It's amazing what you can find in charity shops. We couldn't spend too long though—Comet was letting us know that she was far from comfortable and the whiff was getting unbearable. People kept giving me very funny looks.

Chas paid and then we dashed into Mothercare. There was a sink—I don't think I've ever been so glad to see one—and everything else we might need. The shop assistant happily provided us with a nappy and then we started on the clean-up job. It was worse than I'd imagined. How had Comet managed it? She'd got poo everywhere. I hurled my sweatshirt into the corner of the cubicle in disgust.

'Blimey!' said Chas. 'Where do we start?'

'In the sink,' I said. 'She needs a bath.'

Comet, of course, took exception to that. Boy, did she scream! And kick! There was water everywhere. By the time we'd finished cleaning up, there was a queue of four frantic babies outside.

The baby-carrier was beyond use so Chas went off to beg for a plastic bag into which we stuffed my jacket, my sweatshirt, the carrier and all Comet's dirty things. Comet, who was thoroughly fed up by now, was screaming fit to bust.

'What do we do now?' shouted Chas above the din. 'I'm exhausted.'

I didn't say anything. I could have said a lot—but I didn't.

'All right, Kate,' Chas hollered. 'I admit it. I'm a stupid, thoughtless pig and I ought to have known better. Babies are worse than I thought. Will that do?'

'And I'm a whingeing misery-guts and it really isn't always this bad. OK?

And you're late for Carly.'

We staggered outside and over to the fountain. Comet quietened down as soon as she saw the water.

'You'd better go,' I said.

'Oh, it's OK. Carly will be ages finding things she likes. She'll only want me for a final decision.'

I was just feeling warm all over at the thought of Chas wanting to stay with me, when I caught sight of Nic. He hurried over.

'Kate, what has happened? Where is your jacket? You're shivering!' he said, full of concern. 'And Comet? Where are her clothes? Did you fall in the fountain?'

I laughed. 'No, it's not that bad. I'm fine, Nic. Really.'

But Nic wasn't satisfied. 'But you will freeze!' He stripped off his body-warmer and wrapped it round me. 'Come on. We have some minutes before we meet your mum. I will take you for a hot chocolate and you will tell me what happened.'

'But . . .' I was flummoxed. Nic is lovely and only being kind but this was all wrong. I could see just how Chas would interpret it. At that moment, the last thing I wanted was to be swept away by the Gallic charmer.

'Chas, I . . .' It was too late. Chas's face had gone all closed and wooden.

'See you around then, Kate. You're right. I'm late for Carly.'

And he disappeared into the crowd.

Well, thanks, Nic! Thanks very much indeed!

14

My Mum and the Thanksgiving

Well, I've tried. All week I've tried to get Chas on his own to sort things out but he's really stonewalling me. By last night, I was fed up and when Nic suggested we went to the cinema together, I agreed, even though he had to lend me the money and I've no idea when I'll pay him back.

Big mistake. You can guess what

happened, of course, can't you? Who spotted us in the queue? That's right. Chas and Carly. Chas gave me a look—an 'oh-yes-so-of-course-there's-nothing-going-on-between-you-and-the-French-hunk' sort of look. It never occurred to me that he might mind; I was just mortified that he thought I'd lied to him. But what could I do? I could hardly rush over and say, 'Look, this isn't what you think it is, you know!' Vicky was delighted when I told her this morning.

'You great plonker!' she said. 'He's jealous! Brilliant!'

It is? Well, I suppose it is in one way—maybe he misses me as much as I miss him—but I don't want him to be jealous as in boyfriend-jealous—I just want my friend back!

Anyway, I've too much to do to worry about it now. Tomorrow we've got a Thanksgiving Service for Hayley and Comet so it's all hands on deck. We're having a buffet lunch at the church hall but BTM's convinced some people will want to come back to the house afterwards. That means we've got to make some attempt to tidy it. Any moment now, I'll be on baby duty or be given the Hoover to entertain myself with for an hour or so.

I must say I was a bit puzzled about this Thanksgiving Service bit. I mean, new babies—isn't a christening what you do if you want a party? I decided I'd have to ask Dad again. BTM is perfectly willing to talk about important things, but she's so preoccupied with babies that you can't get any real sense out of her. So Dad would have to deal with it.

'Open the door, Dad! I need to talk to you!'

Dad's head appeared.

'Can't you wait? This is the first uninterrupted bath I've had for a fortnight! Whenever your mum hears the taps running, she thinks it's a golden opportunity to strip off a baby and dump it in for some water-play!'

'Lucky you!' I retorted. 'She can fit both of them in with me!'

Nonetheless, I agreed to wait till he'd finished. I know only too well how he feels not to respect his few moments of peace.

'Why aren't the babies getting christened?' I demanded once he was out and rubbing his hair dry. As predicted, he doesn't have time for the hairdryer these days.

'Aha! You think they don't get *enough* water-play?'

I gave him my 'spare-me-your-humour' look. 'I'm serious,' I said. 'Ben and I were both christened, weren't we?'

'Yes, you know you were. Sorry—your Mum and I have been meaning to talk to you about it—we just haven't had time.'

'Go on then. Tell me. Are they going to be christened later?'

'Well—maybe.' He paused, obviously considering carefully what he was going to say. 'You see, a christening isn't really a name-giving. It's more of a welcome into membership of the church. Pouring water over the baby's head is a sign of that.'

'So?'

'Well, we think that's probably a

190

decision Hayley and Rebekah might prefer to make when they're older. When they've had chance to find out what they believe.'

I pondered for a moment or two, then nodded slowly.

'You're right. I mean, I'm not sure what I believe yet. I'm still—well—experimenting. Even if you did get me christened.'

'Precisely. So this time we're going to have a Thanksgiving Service instead. Just a straightforward, "Thank you God for the lives of these babies." It's quite OK. Anyone can choose to do it—even part-time vicars! Does that meet with your approval?'

I grimaced. 'I'm not sure I *want* to thank God for them, actually. Well, not all the time.'

Dad smiled. 'And neither am I. But we could thank God that they're not an awful lot worse.'

*   *   *

It sounded harmless enough, didn't it? The babies didn't even have to get wet.

Very nice idea. 'Thank you God for these lovely babies, now let's go and have a nice lunch.' Hunky-dory. No sweat.

Ha, ha, ha. We had reckoned without Gran. Such a lot of her time is spent asleep these days that she's nothing like the liability she used to be. Her Sundays out from the nursing home have been one long snore—except when she's playing with the babies. They love her. Give her one to hold and they're happy for ages. She has an endless store of baby rhymes and, of course, Hayley and Comet don't mind if she talks nonsense. You can't leave her alone with one of them in case she falls asleep but she certainly has her uses. And she was really looking forward to the service.

I was surprised then to find her at the church door with Dad, looking tense and tetchy. When I took her arm, she batted at my hand and snapped, 'Leave me alone, Kate! I'm not an invalid, you know!'

'What's the matter?' I hissed at Dad.

He shrugged. 'Something about

some students coming to see her a few days ago. I can't imagine what for and I didn't have time to get the full story from Matron. Anyway, I'm sure she'll snap out of it. She's been looking forward to this.'

I took his word for it and followed Gran down the aisle. There were seats reserved for us on the front pew. This didn't suit Gran at all.

'I can't see anybody from here,' she said crossly.

'But you can see everything,' I said. 'We'll get a brilliant view'

'I didn't say "anything", I said, "anybody". Are you going deaf? I like to see what everyone's wearing.'

I groaned. 'Well, we're stuck with it, I'm afraid, Gran. You'll have to stare at everyone later.'

She looked down her nose at me. 'No one said anything about staring, Kate. It's very rude to stare. What's the matter with you this morning?'

'Let's sit down, Gran,' I said. 'Look. Do you like my new shoes?'

'No. They don't suit you at all. Hideous. You must take after your

193

mother.'

I smiled sweetly and shoved her, still chuntering, into the pew. (Question: do Grannies count as friends you have to love at all times?)

Actually, she had a point about where we were sitting. I was desperate to crane round and see if Chas was there and if he'd brought Carly. We'd almost had a family row about inviting her.

'Look,' said BTM. 'We're inviting all the Petersons. And Chas is almost one of the family . . .'

'Not any more,' I growled.

'I'm sorry?'

'Oh, nothing.'

'Right. Well, I'm sure he'd like to bring Carly along. After all, Ben is bringing Suzie.'

I blinked. 'Excuse me,' I said. 'Ben *is* one of the family. That makes the whole thing quite different. And if Ben's having Suzie and Chas is having Carly, who am I having?'

'Vicky. There, that's perfectly fair.'

'I'm sorry, I don't get this. You like Vicky. You like Suzie. I thought they were *your* guests. Why does Chas get all this special treatment and have to have a guest of his own?'

Dad cleared his throat. 'Jo, darling, I think in the whirl you've been in since you got pregnant, you've missed something rather vital. Carly is not just Carly, she is Cute Carly, Chas's girlfriend, and therefore some of us hate her. You may not have noticed but we haven't actually seen much of Chas in recent weeks.'

'What? But Kate isn't jealous is she? I thought she and Chas were just good friends.'

'*Were*,' said Ben, with emphasis.

'Is this true, Kate?' demanded BTM.

I nodded glumly.

'And *do* you hate Carly?'

'We-e-e-l-l . . .'

'Put it this way, Jo,' said Dad. 'Have you actually met Carly? Properly?'

BTM looked round at our stony faces. 'I think you're all being horrible,' she said. 'And very uncharitable. I'm ashamed of the lot of you. I shall put on the invitation, "Chas plus one" and then he can do what he likes. Honestly!

Sometimes I think you lot read a different Bible from me!'

'Oh yeah?' I said. 'So what gem are you going to quote now?'

She drew herself up regally. 'Humbly consider others better than yourselves,' she said with dignity. 'Think about it, Kate!'

Pah! In your dreams, BTM!

Anyway, I couldn't see Chas, let alone Carly, from where I was sitting, so I just had to wait and see.

The service started pleasantly enough. It was a bit of a squash on the front row with all of us, including Nic, crammed in, plus a box of toys for the babies, the changing bag and Gran's enormous handbag. It was very odd, that bag. I should have got suspicious immediately. Gran's usually very careful about how she dresses, even though she's losing her marbles. She likes things to co-ordinate. I know for a fact that she has at least half a dozen small bags which she's collected over the years. Today she was wearing a very pretty dusky blue dress—so why on earth had she brought a huge brown bag?

We had just finished the first hymn when I found out. Gran sat down, opened the bag, reached in for a handkerchief and . . .

'Aargh!' she shrieked. 'It bit me!'

'Aargh!' I screamed, as something small and furry ran across my lap.

Aargh! It's a rat!' yelled Ben, leaping to his feet and brushing whatever it was onto the floor.

Chaos! Hayley and Comet began to bellow, half the congregation started rummaging around on the floor and the other half stood on the pews and screamed. Gran meanwhile, had gone a ghastly colour and had collapsed in her seat, shaking.

Mum and Dad thrust the babies at Nic and me so they could deal with Gran, while Ben joined most of the other kids on the floor.

Suddenly, there was the most tremendous roll of drums from the music group. Everyone froze. Simon, the vicar, was standing on the steps at the front of the church.

'Thank you,' he said. 'Now that I've

got your attention, if we could all just sit down again quietly, we can continue with the service. If there is a rat loose in the church, then I'm sure our cat Ginger will have it for lunch later. We're all certainly making far too much noise to catch it ourselves and Ginger is an excellent mouser.'

Gran gave a little whimper and sipped the water which Dad had brought her. In a quavering but very clear voice she said, 'Vicar, it wasn't a rat, it was a hamster.'

There was an audible sigh of relief. Simon didn't bat an eyelid. 'Then I'm sure it will turn up, Mrs Lofthouse,' he said. 'Hamsters are like that. Now if we could turn to our service sheets . . .'

We were all—that is all the family and close friends (Chas was there but no Carly—hurray!)—gathered round the vicar for the actual thanksgiving— when I spotted the hamster. Of course, I hadn't been able to concentrate on the service at all. I just kept wondering why on earth Gran had a hamster in her handbag. Anyway, I spotted him. There are wooden rails built out from the sides of the church either side of the steps where we were standing. Harry the Hamster was perched on the end of one, pretending he was a meerkat. He looked very interested in the proceedings.

I bided my time. He didn't look as if he was going anywhere. I waited till Simon told us all to sit down and then I leapt.

Wham! Someone else had leapt too. Our heads met in mid-flight and I fell back, blinded.

More chaos. I could hear it through the roaring in my ears. I clutched my pounding head and struggled slowly to my feet. A man I barely knew gave me a hand. In front of me, my family and friends were bunched round Chas, who was lying motionless at the foot of the steps, blood oozing from a gash at the side of his head. Dad (who's good at this sort of thing) was feeling his neck for a pulse. I took one look at Chas's white face and ran.

I couldn't run far—my own head was far too painful and I felt sick and dizzy. I collapsed in the corner of the graveyard and began retching violently. When I'd stopped, I didn't feel better; I felt dreadful and began to sob. If Chas was dead, he'd died thinking I cared more about Nic than about him.

'No God—no!' I could hear myself babbling. 'He mustn't be dead. Please God, don't let him be dead. I've been so horrible—but please don't let him be dead.'

I was rocking backwards and forwards, holding my stomach, my face a sodden mass of tears, when Mum found me.

'Mum,' I croaked. 'Why aren't you with the babies?'

Mum put her arms round me. 'What a stupid thing to say,' she said. 'I do have another daughter as well, you know. One that needs me a good deal more than they do right now, by the look of things.'

'But they need you all the time!' I wailed.

Mum hugged me closer, despite the snot and her new outfit. 'Oh dear,' she said. 'I can't have been being a very good mum, if you think I can't look for you when you're half-concussed. Dear me, you didn't have to run this far to be sick, you know!'

'Mum, tell me quickly. Chas . . . is he?'

'He'll be fine, Kate. He's come round now. Needs a few stitches in that gash though. You were lucky. Poor old Chas landed head first on the edge of a step. What on earth possessed you both to leap for that hamster? He was perfectly happy.'

I couldn't answer—I just cried and cried and cried.

'Kate, Kate, what is all this?' said Mum, in bewilderment. 'You must have *really* shaken yourself up!' She was holding me very close.

I shook my head. It hurt. ' 'Tisn't that,' I said. 'It's just . . . oh, I thought Chas was dead! And we haven't been speaking all week and I . . . oh, I couldn't bear it!'

Mum said nothing. She didn't dismiss what I'd said. She just held me in her arms, kneeling on the muddy ground, until I'd finished crying.

I was dragged off to hospital too. Dad thought I ought to be checked over since I'd been so sick and was still distinctly groggy. Chas was ready to go when I got back to the church. Mrs Charming Peterson was just tucking him into their Land Rover with a travel rug. He was very green but that was a hundred times better than the deathly white he had been. I stumbled over to him.

'Chas,' I croaked. 'I'm so glad you're not dead.'

Chas half-opened an eye. 'Me too,' he said and made a feeble attempt at a grin.

Then there was an argument about how I was to get to hospital. Mum loudly protested that she wanted to take me but, as Dad pointed out, she had a party to attend to and the twins might need feeding.

Mum was adamant though. 'You can phone if you really need me,' she said. 'I want to know my oldest daughter is going to be all right.'

So it was settled. Dad and Mrs Charming would hold the fort (right up her street) while Mum and Mr Peterson did the hospital run.

Neither Chas nor I felt well enough to talk, but I did manage to get out of Mum where the hamster had come from.

'It was part of a research project,' she explained. 'A group from the university is studying the effect of keeping a pet on life-expectancy and Gran's home had been asked to take part. A third of the patients were given hamsters, a third were given potted plants and a third weren't given anything at all. Gran was in the plant group but she wanted a hamster—so she stole one from the lady next door. It's as simple as that.'

'Pikes,' I muttered. 'What a crazy idea!'

'Well, not that crazy—except that if I got nothing when everyone else got hamsters and plants, I'd assume no one loved me and drop dead immediately!'

At the hospital, I was X-rayed and sent home. We were lucky. There wasn't a long queue. It felt great to have Mum to myself for a while—almost worth the bang on the head. I guess I hadn't realized just how much I'd resented the way the babies had preoccupied her—in fact, I had to admit that accounted for a large part of my grumpiness since she'd got pregnant—but I didn't want her to miss the party. I didn't enjoy it myself, I'm afraid: in fact, I hid in my room most of the time—but at least I got out of the clearing up.

And what about Chas? Well, he was all right too, of course. He was kept in overnight for observation but released in the morning. Mum took me round to see him in the afternoon.

'We'll be at least an hour,' she said, as she and Nic packed the babies into their carriers for a healthy walk across the fields. 'So you've plenty of time to say whatever you need to say. Have fun!'

Chas was watching TV in the lounge but as soon as he saw me, he got up. 'Come on,' he said. 'Let's go to the outhouse. I don't want Mum barging in, fussing over me. There's something I've got to tell you.'

Slowly, we made our way across the yard. As he opened the door of his den, I wondered if I'd see a transformation. Would Carly have made him tidy up?

It was a huge relief to find it as messy as ever. He caught my eye.

'You're right,' he said. 'Carly couldn't bear it.'

'Couldn't?' I said, a catch in my breath.

He grinned. 'That's what I've got to tell you. I've split up with her. And I feel fantastic—apart from my head!'

I felt like flinging my arms round him in relief but decided he might misunderstand. 'But why?' I stammered.

He shrugged. 'I'm fed up with her. She's so fussy. And so possessive. She couldn't bear me being friends with you. She didn't even like me spending any time with Ben. And really, she's only interested in . . . well . . .' He stopped, blushing.

'Oh, I don't know,' I said charitably. 'She's interested in clothes too—

205

and dancing.'

Chas laughed. 'Oh Kate,' he said. 'I have missed you. But you were a grumpy old bat for months.'

'Sorry,' I said. 'But I felt awful.'

'So what's changed? Is it because of Nic?'

'Will you shut up about Nic? There is nothing going on between me and Nic! Believe me!'

Chas raised an eyebrow. 'Are you sure? It didn't look that way last Saturday. I could just see myself finishing with Carly and finding I'd suddenly got no friends!'

'You'd still have Ben. And Vicky. And if I ever do have a boyfriend, I'm not going to let it stop me having other friends. But anyway, Nic is very sweet and kind—and just like an older brother. And even if he wasn't, I wouldn't be going out with him. Everyone else might be suffering from raging hormones—but I'm not.'

I paused, embarrassed about what I wanted to say.

'Go on,' said Chas encouragingly.

I smiled. It was wonderful to be back

on speaking terms.

'It's just that the whole baby thing was really hard,' I said awkwardly. 'I felt God must hate me. I mean, how could there possibly be anything good about twins? And just when I'd been getting on so well with Mum. And then there was you and Carly and Ben and Suzie. My whole life seemed to be falling apart.'

'Sorry. I wasn't a lot of help, was I?'

'No. You were useless. All that, "Now, Kate, you're not being very positive about this." I felt like beating you to a pulp. And don't go thinking it's all better now. It still does my head in. Hayley and Comet can be a real pain—but I do love them. They weren't *such* a bad idea, after all.'

'But you *are* still my friend? Even though I'm useless?' Chas had that pleading look—the one I can't resist.

'Of course I am, you wally. When I thought you'd died yesterday, I felt like dying too. I've never been so relieved in my life to see anyone looking green.'

'Well, that's all right then,' said Chas, with a big smile. 'Sorted. Phew!' He opened a battered old tin. 'Look—I've got some chocolate biscuits to celebrate.'

'Oh, honestly!' I said, taking two. 'You don't change, do you?'

But he has, of course. And so has Ben. And I suppose I'm changing too. But who cares? As Chas says, we're sorted. For now, at any rate. After all, a friend loves at all times.